SUNFLOWERS

' ... Three children get caught up in adult hatreds dating from World War II, an aunt who fell in love, a grandfather who nearly killed to stop her love and the sunflower house where it all happened. Through the dreamy heat of summer dangerous emotions well up ...'

British Book News

'Joan Lingard is a born novelist and her *Snake among the Sunflowers* has the essential qualities of a good novel: plot suspense, characters, good dialogue, vivid setting (this time in the south of France).'

Manchester Evening News

Snake among the Sunflowers

Joan Lingard

CANONGATE · KELPIES

First published 1977 by Hamish Hamilton Children's Books
90 Great Russell Street, London WC1D 3PT
First published in Kelpies 1984

Cover illustration by Jill Downie

Printed in Great Britain
by Redwood Burn Ltd, Trowbridge, Wiltshire

ISBN 0 86241 070 3

*The publishers acknowledge the financial assistance
of the Scottish Arts Council in the
publication of this volume*

CANONGATE PUBLISHING LTD
17 JEFFREY STREET, EDINBURGH EH1 1DR

CONTENTS

FOR JENNY

with love

'Look before you leap,
For snakes among sweet flowers do creep.'
(Old English Proverb)

1

Strangers in the Sunflower House

SOPHIE RAN AT full tilt down the steep road towards the bottom of the valley. At the foot she paused, gasping. Whilst she gulped for breath she kept her eyes fixed high up on the other side of the valley, her destination, where her house stood, screened by trees, where her brother and sister would be basking like lizards in the sun, blissfully ignorant of what she had just seen. It was not that she had seen anything particularly horrifying in itself to reduce her to such a state of shocked excitement: it was that what she had seen had been so totally unexpected.

She must move on, climb the rough winding track overhung with clutching brambles and carry the news to Claudine and Paul. For a moment she relished the vision of their startled faces. "*You must have imagined it, Sophie!*" But no, she had not: she had seen and heard with her eyes and ears, quite clearly and unmistakably. Her legs moved rhythmically, gradually picking up speed again. The need to tell was greater than the need to rest.

Up above, but not visible from the road below, lay Claudine and Paul, as Sophie had suspected. They were lying in long grass partly shaded by the branches of a chestnut tree.

Paul was thinking that the scent of cantaloups coming up from his grandfather's farm below was making him feel drunk. It was a very strong, heady smell. He had never been drunk, not exactly;

I

the nearest he had been was when he felt a warm glow of happiness after drinking a couple of glasses of the old man's full-bodied red wine. With his eyes closed against the glare of the sun, he imagined a cantaloup cut in half, the two pieces orange and luscious, dripping with juice, and his mouth watered.

It was hot in the Lot, Claudine was thinking, the words repeating themselves in her mind like a hypnotic chant, almost as insistent as the steady tic-tic-tic of the cicadas. Seeking moisture, she plucked a grass and sank her teeth into it, but it felt and tasted like straw. She threw it aside and rolled over on to her back, wishing that she could plunge to the bottom of an ice-cold lake.

They were in the Lot and Garonne, a region of South-West France, where it was usually hot in summer-time, but especially so this summer. It was exceptional, said everyone, including their grandparents who thrived on heat and did not come from the brisk shores of the North Sea, as their grandchildren did. Their daughter – the children's mother – had been born and raised on the farm in the valley but had married a Scotsman by the name of Grant and gone to live in exile, in Edinburgh. And every year the Grants made the journey from the South-East of Scotland to the South-West of France.

From across the valley the church bell began to toll. Madame Grenier, ancient and hunched, a little dusty-looking in her eternal navy-blue and white spotted dress and elderly straw hat, would be pulling on the rope. Twelve times she would pull, to let the world know it was midday. The sound echoed throughout the length of the valley. Things were falling into place again, thought Paul; the pattern was set, nothing was changed. He liked patterns and order, and the idea of events returning and repeating in a cycle. He did not want to come back one summer and find that everything – anything – was changed.

When Sophie heard the bell she stopped for another rest. It seemed impossible to ignore it, to carry on without some token of acknowledgement. They always paused in whatever they were doing at the first stroke to count the other eleven. Seven, eight . . .

2

She held out her hands, trying to catch the vibrations on the air. Nine, ten . . . In the wood on her right she could see her father standing still also, listening. Eleven, twelve. The last note lingered. She strained her ears until she could hear only the cicadas and the warbling of a bird close by. Her father had resumed work again; he was stooping to clear the tangled undergrowth under the damson trees. She did not call out to him, not wanting to delay any longer the bringing of the news about the sunflower house to Claudine and Paul. The house was on the other side of the valley, below the church, and they had given it that name because it was surrounded by sunflowers, big tall ones with huge yellow heads that turned the garden into a mass of gold every year.

Unaware that the present was about to be disturbed, Paul was thinking about his future. In four years' time, when he was eighteen, he intended to come and work on the farm, and then, sometime in the even further away future, when his grandfather died – when he was a very old man of course – he, Paul, would run the farm. It was a good farm, prosperous, fertile, well-ordered.

Claudine's mind was travelling in a similar direction. It was always thus, during their first few days in the valley each summer. How lovely it was, they murmured, and how nice it would be not to have to go home at the end of summer . . . Claudine intended to settle in France too when she was eighteen, which for her would come in three years' time now. She planned to live in Paris with her Aunt Nicole, her mother's younger sister. Aunt Nicole was full of mystery, or gave the impression that she was; she smelled of expensive perfume, swished in silky clothes and talked English in a sexy voice. She lived in an apartment on the Left Bank, the only place to live in Paris, Claudine considered. What did she intend to do in Paris? Paul was always asking annoying questions like that, which Claudine dismissed as details. She would find something. Her ambition was to be an artist, paint, have a studio. And starve, said Paul. Paris was full of people with romantic notions, according to him.

A shutter at the side of the house creaked outwards, turning their

3

heads a fraction. Their mother, stretching and looking remarkably like someone who had just woken up, stood at the window.

"You shouldn't be lying in the grass. There might be a snake."

Sophie had sighted a snake the day before in the long grass at the side of the house. Long grass grew abundantly everywhere, in spite of the fact that their father spent a large part of the summer wielding a scythe, and the grass spent the rest of the year springing back up again. Their mother would never have objected to them lying under the tree if it hadn't been for yesterday's snake. Brown and yellow it had been, striped, and enormous, according to Sophie, who was good at sighting things. Little would go past her in life, said their father.

Neither Claudine nor Paul moved; their mother withdrew. In all the years that they had been coming to this valley they had only ever seen three snakes. It seemed unlikely another would appear today, or even that the same one should be sighted twice. It was against all the odds, said Paul.

All the grey-blue shutters stood wide open now, flung back against the whitewashed walls of the L-shaped, one-storeyed building. The roof was of red pantiles. Behind were the old cowsheds, where they stored their bicycles, and to the left, the *pigeonnier*. There were no pigeons in habitation any more though it still smelt of the birds. They hated standing inside the *pigeonnier* looking up at the perches where the birds had roosted, cramped together, getting fattened up, awaiting the moment when they would be ready for the farmer's table.

When they had bought the house three years ago it had been very dilapidated. Since then they had been doing it up, or their father had, with a bit of help here and there when he could muster it. The trouble was that when they came here they never felt very energetic, not as energetic as they felt back in Edinburgh making plans.

"Here comes Sophie," murmured Claudine, who could hear her feet on the drive and did not need to lift her head. "Imagine, running!"

4

"How can she, in this heat?"

"Youth! Anyway, she is incapable of being still."

Sophie was almost upon them now, flying. She looked excited, as if about to burst. But then she often did. Her excitement seldom excited them.

"You'll never guess —" She could hardly speak.

"Sit down, Sophie," said Paul. "Take a deep breath."

"And count to a hundred," said Claudine, yawning.

Sophie did not sit down. She gulped and said, "There's people in the sunflower house!"

Immediately, Claudine and Paul sat up and regarded their young sister with disbelief.

"What did you say?" demanded Claudine.

"People in the —" Sophie was still short of breath.

"Are you sure?" asked Paul. "How do you know?"

"I saw them. Well — I almost did. But the shutters are wide open and there's a car at the side of the house."

Claudine and Paul looked at one another. Since ever they could remember the sunflower house had been shut, and as far as they knew no one had lived there for twenty years or more. No one seemed to know who owned it or why it was closed up. They thought of it as their own. They had always gone there to play and still frequented it even though they, Claudine and Paul, anyway, had passed the stage of playing.

"Someone must have bought it," said Claudine slowly, frowning, unable quite to comprehend it. Was it really possible?

"We won't be able to go there any more," said Paul.

"Unless we make friends," said Sophie hopefully, scratching one of the many bites on her legs. She was beginning to turn brown already, after only three days. She never went inside or stayed in the shade unless forced to.

"It wouldn't be the same," said Claudine. "It wouldn't be *ours*."

Their father was coming up the drive. He looked damp and hot.

"Don't sit out in the sun too long now! You especially, Paul."

Paul was fair-skinned, like his father, and the sun blistered them easily, making them moan and groan in the night. Claudine and Sophie were olive-skinned, as their mother was, and they could soak up sun and turn brown without going a fiery red first. "Unfair!" declared the male members of the family. Mr Grant had started to take on a bright shade of red, especially across the front of his feet. Every summer he burnt his feet. It was a family joke.

"I'm hungry. Don't know about you lot."

Paul got up. "I'll give you a hand this afternoon, Dad." He felt guilty, looking at his father's flushed face.

"O.K., if you feel like it." Mr Grant always said that he did not want to turn his children's holiday into a labour camp, so it was up to them if they helped or not. Not everyone enjoyed Doing-It-Yourself, as he did.

They walked, all four, up the last bit of the drive to the front of the house, around which wisteria grew in profusion covering the white wall with purple blossom. Mrs Grant was setting lunch out on the table under the blue and white striped umbrella on the terrace. Long crusty loaves, paté, tomatoes, cheese, patisserie, and a bottle of wine. Their French relations ate enormous meals at midday: they partook of hot soup from large china tureens, ate stuffed tomatoes, veal stew, or beef soaked in wine. Their grandmother did not approve of the Grants' way of eating, for they ate their biggest meal of the day in the evening, often quite late, sitting in the dining room with the windows wide open on to the dark night. She said it was not good for the stomach to take heavy food on so late. Her daughter had forgotten the customs of her country. Her daughter protested that when they were at home it was not convenient to have a meal at midday, for neither the children nor her husband came home at lunch-time. That made *Grand'mère* humph. People should come back to their own home in the middle of the day. She had come once to the Eastern coast of Scotland. She had come in an unusually wet November, full of North Sea haar and the mournful sound of foghorns bleating on the Firth of Forth.

6

She had not liked it. Their grandfather had not come and never would.

The Grants sat down to eat. Mr Grant ate heartily, and Sophie, whose appetite seldom waned, kept pace with him, but Paul and Claudine had unusually little appetite that day. They were thinking about the sunflower house and the people inside it.

After lunch, they cleared away and washed the dishes.

Then, without a word, they left the house and went down the drive together, or, at least, Paul and Claudine walked side by side, but Sophie ran ahead, like a dog, coming back at intervals to offer bits of information just recalled. For example: she had heard voices in the house. Men's voices.

When they emerged at the bottom of the drive on to the road they were able to see their grandparents' farmhouse on their right. The verandah was empty. The old folk would be having an after-lunch siesta in the cool dim interior.

The children took the steep narrow road that climbed over the back of the hill, past the sunflower house and the church. They slowed as they neared the house, and listened. There was no sound of any person, only that of cicadas and birds, which seemed tireless and in no need of siestas. And if they listened very hard they became conscious of the steady hum of dozens of small insects. Now that they were almost at the house they were having doubts about whether they actually wanted to see the new inhabitants or not. Paul and Claudine's steps lagged, but Sophie forged ahead with resolution.

It was necessary to go right up to the gate to be able to see the garden and get a good look at the house for the front hedges were wildly overgrown and the trees were thick and unpruned. Sophie was right! She was, in fact, seldom wrong, although her sister and brother would never have admitted it, to her. The shutters stood wide open, the front door also, and there tucked in at the side of the house was a small red car.

"Well!" said Paul. There seemed to be nothing else to say.

The house was two-storeyed, of honey-coloured stone, with a pantiled roof that had been faded by the sun to a pinkish-brown. The sunflowers were in full, glorious bloom. It seemed like a miracle to come back each year and find them growing again. They were annuals, but they appeared to seed themselves. As Paul pointed out, they did not have much problem with frost in this part of the world. They dreaded that, one spring, there might be a particularly bad late frost which would kill off the seeds. So far, it had not happened. "Fingers crossed," said Sophie, crossing as many as were possible, whenever the topic was discussed.

Bedding lay over the window sills.

"I expect they're very busy," said Claudine. "It must have been pretty stuffy in there, shut up for twenty years." She spoke mournfully.

When their parents had decided to buy some property in the valley instead of staying with the grandparents every summer, the children had begged them to buy this house.

"It's quite out of the question," Mrs Grant had said, rather abruptly.

"We don't know how to contact the owner," Mr Grant had added.

Did *Grand-père* not know? they had asked, finding it difficult to think that he would not. He knew most people's business around here.

"No!" Their mother had been unusually and strangely sharp. "Anyway, we like the old house on the hill, and the view over the valley."

"I thought you liked to be secluded," said Claudine. She had heard her mother say so the day before when she was reading estate agents' literature. "I've heard you say so."

"I do. But that house is too hemmed in." And their own house benefited from many more hours sunshine by being high up. "Goodness knows but we need as much sunshine as we can get after ten months in Edinburgh!" Mrs Grant liked to speak witheringly of that city but she was, in truth, very fond of it.

It suited her temperament, Claudine had often heard her say to her friends there. This pastoral scene, with her father still behaving as if he owned her even after sixteen years of marriage, would certainly not. "Anyway," she had added, in a voice that was intended to clinch and end the argument, "that house is too small. There are only four rooms and none are large, apart from the kitchen."

"How do you know? Have you been inside?"

"I may have been."

May! That was too loose a statement for Claudine to let pass. "What do you mean – may?"

"I expect I was as a child. I have been in most houses in the valley at some time or other."

Then Mrs Grant had shrugged. Claudine found her mother's shrugs infuriating. They were her way of ending an argument by inferring that it was all too boring and she was no longer interested. It was a way of escaping the point, Claudine thought.

"But four rooms –"

"Claudine, I do not like that house!" Her mother's word had been final and Claudine had known it.

It was not that they did not like their own house, they did; it was just that for years they had coveted the sunflower house, had imagined owning it, moving in, opening up the shutters. And now, someone else was doing that.

"Should we go and say hello?" suggested Sophie, her hand on the gate.

"Certainly not," said her brother and sister simultaneously.

At that moment a boy, around the age of the two older Grants, appeared at the front door carrying a rug. He looked startled when he saw the three pairs of eyes staring at him.

"*Bonjour*," said Claudine politely.

"*Bonjour*," he replied. He was not French.

Sophie repeated the greeting and smiled broadly upon him, whilst fingering the gate catch. For a moment it looked as if he might retreat backwards, and then he advanced hesitantly into the garden, half looking at them, half looking away, and began to flap the rug about self-consciously.

"Come on," muttered Paul, edging away.

"Nice day," said Sophie, in French.

"Yes," said the boy with the rug, giving it another feeble flap. He sneezed. The rug was thick with dust.

"It's a lovely house," said Claudine, pointing behind him, so that there would be no misunderstanding, so that she could bring the house to the centre of attention.

He glanced back at the house, glad perhaps to have an excuse to escape their eyes.

Sophie leant on the gate, Claudine stood behind her with her hand on her sister's shoulder. They showed no signs of moving. Paul waited a few steps away, wishing that his sisters were not so insatiably curious. He often complained that he could not go any-where with them. Claudine especially was terrible, even though she appeared on the surface to be less curious than Sophie. She tended to push Sophie forward, to make her the spearhead of the attack, as it were. Sophie would smile, open her dark eyes wide and, engagingly, ask a simple question, which would enable Claudine to come forward and make use of the opening by slipping in a more penetrating query. She liked to get to the bottom of things, she declared, and could see nothing wrong with that. Sophie, with her seeming innocence and lack of self-consciousness, was essential to her in situations where it might be unseemly for a fif-teen-year-old to pry. Together they were formidable.

"Come on," murmured Paul again, but they were not paying any attention to him. Their eyes and ears were focused straight ahead.

For years Claudine had wanted to get to the bottom of the mystery of this house. Was there a mystery? Paul sometimes asked. It was merely a shut-up house. There were shut-up houses every-where, even in their street in Edinburgh. But no one knew who owned it or why it was shut up, Claudine objected. Someone knew, countered Paul. Precisely! That, according to Claudine, constituted a mystery: the identity of that someone. They had contemplated many theories, even Paul, whilst sitting under the old fig tree with sunflowers at their feet; idly contemplated, that was, for the warmth and peace and drone of insects were not conducive to incisive investigation. Drowsily, and peacefully, they had discussed the possibilities of a dead body inside the shuttered house (wouldn't it smell? – they were not sure), a haul of stolen jewellery (thieves languishing in prison waiting to return to collect), a war criminal holed up (starving?), spies who came and went at night (playing at statues during the day), a descendant of the murdered Czar of Russia (Anastasia's daughter?). Sometimes they went on and elaborated, built up a story, a list of characters with names, identities and descriptions. When they were younger they had imagined fairies, princesses, witches and wizards, gradually moving, as Paul said, to harder characters.

"Why don't you break open a shutter?" Sophie had suggested one day. "Then we could see."

Claudine and Paul had been horrified.

And now the house was open, the shutters back. The mysteries were at an end. Anastasia's daughter could not be in there, or a jewel thief, or even a dead body, presumably.

"It's good weather for cleaning," said Claudine. "House cleaning. Scrubbing floors." She made a scrubbing movement with her hand. "Airing beds and things."

"Yes," said the boy.

Claudine smiled, moving a little to the right of Sophie, so that she too now leant against the gate.

"You are just moving in?" she said in a conversational tone, speaking slowly and positively so that the boy could follow if his grasp of French was poor.

"No."

Perhaps he could say nothing but yes or no. Perhaps he did not even understand what they said to him. He was not British: they could tell that. They found that they could always tell.

"No? You're not moving in?" said Claudine.

"We are just moving out," said the boy in stilted but careful French.

2

Disturbances at 'Les Rossignols'

"CHRISTIAN!" A VOICE, a man's voice, called from within.

Christian nodded at the girls, mumbling something vague and inaudible, and then, clutching the rug, returned indoors.

"*Au revoir*," called Sophie clearly after him.

The door of the house closed.

"Well, what do you know?" said Claudine.

They walked slowly back down the road. Sophie stayed beside them this time.

"Imagine!" she said. Her black eyes were even rounder than usual. "Do you think they've been living in there all along?"

"Don't be silly," said Paul. "How could they?"

"But what did he mean then? Just moving out?"

Neither Claudine nor Paul could tell her. They said little more as they continued down the hill. They were thinking.

At the farm gate they met their grandfather seated high up on his tractor. He leant down to kiss the girls and to shake hands with Paul. How nice it was to have them all back once again in the valley!

"Are you coming with me, Paul?"

At once Paul climbed up beside him. He never needed to be asked twice to accompany his grandfather. The tractor moved off along the road, the girls went inside to find their grandmother.

Paul and his grandfather talked of farm matters, of the cows and their milk yield that morning. The old man was totally a man of the countryside, a farmer, and a hunter and fisher also. He had taught Paul to fish and was always lamenting that they left before the hunting season began in September. Paul's father, not being keen on the idea of guns and shooting animals himself, was just as glad about that, but his wife had said that he should let the boy hunt if he wished, that it was very much a French thing, taking part in the hunt. And after all, was Paul himself not half French?

Seated on the tractor, talking to his grandfather, Paul forgot all about the sunflower house and the boy with the rug. They passed fields full of peaches, apricots, cantaloups, tomatoes, corn, and, of course, plums. This was a region for plums, and famous for prunes and prune liqueur. When visitors called his grandmother served prune liqueur in special china cups that she had been given on her wedding day.

Sitting on the geranium-potted verandah of their grandparents' house, eating slices of dripping cantaloup, the girls had not forgotten the sunflower house, nor the boy with the strange accent. Claudine only half listened as her grandmother talked. She was telling them about her sister, their Great-Aunt Eulalie, who was a widow and lived alone in Agen. Every now and then they had to go and visit her in her faded, shuttered house, where the sun was never allowed to penetrate in case it might do damage to the carpets or furniture, which, regardless of such care, were gradually being drained of all colour, due, simply, to the passage of time. Claudine and Sophie could only think of the house which had been shuttered for twenty years and into which the sun was now streaming.

Claudine finished her cantaloup, wiped her hands on her shorts and eyed her grandmother. Although approaching seventy, *Grand'mère* had a remarkably unlined face, smooth and serene. She was the calmest person the children had ever known. Their own mother was inclined to get flustered, to fly into a rage at times, and then spout at them in a long torrent of French. But they

14

had never heard their grandmother raise her voice or get excited. She strayed seldom from home and was most content when in her garden amongst her flowers or sitting on her verandah.

"*Grand'mère*," began Claudine hesitantly.

"Yes, my child?"

"You know the house half way up the hill – ?"

Grand'mère looked away, out beyond the garden, over to the fields, to where the cows were grazing. "Your Aunt Nicole is due tomorrow," she said. "That should please you, eh? She will bring news of Paris with her."

That normally would have pleased the children, still did, but their minds were more on something else at that moment. Their grandmother now began to talk about Aunt Nicole and how well she was doing in her work as an interior designer. She had flair and taste and people liked her ideas. There was no chance to revert to the subject of the sunflower house, not that Claudine considered that they had ever been on it. It had always gone this way when she had tried to raise the matter. *Grand'mère* had always refused to acknowledge that she had heard.

They spent the long hot afternoon at the farm, and when the sun was dropping and the grain beginning to smell strong and heady, they set back up the drive to their own house. As soon as they drew near they smelt the tantalising smells of dinner cooking. Their father was sitting on the terrace reading and drinking an aperitif.

"Set the table, will you?" called their mother through the open window.

They went in. Paul was there, cutting onions for the salad. Sophie lifted a pot lid, almost burning her fingers. Beef and mushrooms cooked in red wine. Delicious!

"I'm starved."

"Soon be ready." Their mother hummed as she put the last touches to their meal.

Claudine and Paul set the long table in front of the two windows. The shutters were open, they could see the garden from where they ate. The house had one large main room, very long, about thirty feet or more, and low-ceilinged. It had a big wide fireplace on the wall opposite the two windows and alongside that there was a half-door, which looked out on to the old cowshed behind. In this room, they cooked, ate, and sat.

"Dinner-time!" called their mother.

The children were at the table even as she spoke. They started with cantaloup, followed by the beef stew with rice, with green beans and a tomato and onion salad, then they had cheese and apricot tart. They ate contentedly and for a long time, Paul and Claudine being allowed a glass of wine to accompany their meal, and Sophie an inch or so, with water in it, at which she always complained loudly. Through the open windows came the smell of roses and geraniums, and underlying the sweet scent of the flowers was the thick smell of the grain from further up the valley. It was very much an evening smell.

Sophie finished her second piece of tart and said, eyeing her mother and father in turn, with an air of innocence that only she had perfected, "We saw the sunflower house people today."

Their mother frowned, and turned quickly on Sophie. "What are you talking about?"

"There are people living in the house. We saw them this afternoon. Didn't we, Paul?"

Paul shrugged. "We saw a boy."

"Did you speak to him?"

"I said *bonjour*," said Sophie. "And Claudine talked to him."

"What did he have to say for himself then?" Their father sounded unconcerned, unlike their mother.

"Nothing. He didn't speak French very well."

"How odd." Mrs Grant was eyeing her husband. He shrugged, and she said, addressing him, "They must have bought it."

"Sounds like it." Mr Grant poured his wife more wine.

Claudine said, "The boy said they were just moving out."

"But how can they since they have not been in before?" asked Mrs Grant.

"That's what we'd like to know."

"It's like a riddle," said Sophie, swinging her legs beneath the table.

"So they weren't French?" asked their father in a casual way suggesting that he was really not particularly interested, but somehow they sensed that he was.

"They're German," said Paul.

"German!" exclaimed their mother. "*Mon Dieu!*"

Claudine turned to Paul. "How do you know?"

"Their car, stupid! The registration plate."

She had been too interested in the boy to look at the car. Claudine and Paul kept their eyes on their parents, trying to read what was in their faces but could not. They seemed disturbed by the news, but why should they be? What could the sunflower house have to do with them?

"Do you mind if they're German, Mother?" asked Claudine.

"No, no, of course not," she said hurriedly.

"But you sounded—"

"Oh, it's just your grandfather." She threw up her hands. "You know what he's like."

They did, and had often heard his views on Germans. He had fought with the Resistance movement during the war, been one of its heroes.

From 1940 onward this area had been part of what was known as Vichy France, so-called because it was administered from the spa town of Vichy. The government, which was anti-republic and accepted the German occupation of the rest of France, was regarded as a traitorous body by many Frenchmen, amongst whom numbered their grandfather. For the first two years he had operated as a member of the Resistance from home, but in November 1942 the Germans occupied Vichy France also and so he was forced to flee to the Pyrenees where he had a sister living. There he led one of the encampments, or groups, known as the Maquis. He performed many daring acts of sabotage, and was extremely brave. His hatred of the Germans was strengthened when his younger brother, also a

17

Resistance fighter, was captured, tortured and subsequently shot by the enemy. So, even after all these years – more than thirty – he could neither forget nor forgive. His grandchildren did not understand his bitterness against *all* Germans, but their parents said that they must be tolerant and try to realize how deeply his experiences had affected him. Thirty years might seem a long time to them, but it was not to him.

"Well, he doesn't have to like Germans if he doesn't want to, does he?" said Paul stoutly. He was always *Grand'père's* chief defender.

He excused himself and got up, going to stand by the half-door to look out into the darkness behind the house.

"Do you *have* to like everybody, Daddy?" asked Sophie.

"Difficult question, Sophie."

The discussion was at an end, for they had a visitor. It was *Grand-père* himself, puffing a little from his climb up the drive. He would never take his time, had to go everywhere on the trot. He came in now, wiping the sweat from his brow with his handkerchief. "*Bonsoir, tout le monde.*" He kissed his daughter on both cheeks and then his two granddaughters. No matter how many times a day he met them he would kiss them.

Mr Grant asked him to sit down and poured a glass of wine. The old man was still puffing and looked almost done in. Of course he was not getting any younger, as their Edinburgh grandmother would have put it. He drank the glass of wine at a gulp, held it out to be refilled. Back home Sophie bragged that her grandfather was the biggest wine drinker in all of France. Claudine said she shouldn't go around saying such a thing for *Grand-père* could never be that. He had told them about some farmers he knew who could drink twenty bottles in one day! He was not such a stickler for the truth as his wife was, so they were never sure if the things he told them were *exactly* right. They were right in essence, said their mother, if not in detail.

"And what difficult question was it you were asking, Sophie?" asked *Grand-père*.

"I just wanted to know if you had to like everybody."

"Like everybody? Certainly not! It is not possible. Or practical."

He then said that he wanted to talk to his daughter and her husband. "Alone, if you please. This is private business."

That was not unusual. All their grandfather's business was private. He loved secrecy and intrigue.

Paul left the room first, followed by Sophie, and finally Claudine, who went reluctantly. She considered that at fifteen she should be thought of primarily as an adult and hated to be banned from family conferences. They went, all three, into the girls' room and sat on Claudine's bed. Paul suggested a game of cards.

"Come away from there, Sophie," said Paul. She had her ear laid against the door. "You know it's wrong to eavesdrop."

She did not move. "I can't really hear. They're at the other end of the room and they're whispering."

"What have they to whisper about?" said Claudine thoughtfully.

"They're probably just speaking quietly," said Paul. "Not whispering!"

"The sunflower house! That's what they're talking about."

"Are you sure?" Paul lifted his head: he had been in the middle of dealing for a game of sevens.

"Mm, I think so."

"Curiouser and curiouser," said Claudine.

Paul called to them to come and play; they went.

"I've been thinking," he said, lifting his cards and frowning at them. "Those German people might easily have been there for a month or so. We're not to know that they weren't."

"They weren't there when we first arrived," said Claudine. "That's three days ago."

"That's true." He shifted a card around, made a run of three.

"And they weren't there yesterday. They can't have been. The place was closed, you know it was. And not a thing had been moved since last summer." They had sat on the old seat in the

19

garden and had a picnic, and they had commented that nothing was changed. They would have known if people had been in residence: there would have been signs.

"They must have come this morning," said Sophie.

"Stop looking at my cards, Sophie!" Paul held them closer to his chest.

It would be odd if the people had only come that morning and were getting ready to leave already, commented Claudine. Paul suggested that they might have hated the house on sight; they might have bought it through an estate agent without seeing it. How could they hate such a nice sweet house? demanded Claudine. Paul said that it was quite possible. People were odd, after all, and not everybody liked the same things. Just because they liked the house so much was no reason to presume that everyone else would. They might have found it closed in, decided they would prefer to have a house with a view, like theirs. The boy's father might suffer from claustrophobia.

"Mummy and Daddy don't seem to like it," said Sophie. "Do they?"

"I wonder why," said Claudine. She drummed her fingers on the table. Their mother was infuriating to question, she was so elusive.

They began to play their game of cards, forgetting for a little while the subject of the sunflower house, though at the back of their minds the thoughts still ran, though less so in Sophie's case.

She won three games in a row.

"You'll be unlucky at love," said Claudine.

"I don't care. I'd rather win games."

"You can come out now," called their father, releasing them. *Grand-père* was about to leave. He said goodnight, and Mr Grant accompanied him down the drive.

"What did he want?" asked Claudine.

Their mother was off-hand. Oh, nothing very much. Although on the other hand it might be serious. His old sister who still lived in the Pyrenees, and of whom he was very fond, was ill. He couldn't go himself to see her, so he wanted their mother to go and take Aunt Nicole, when she arrived, with her.

"So that was why he came?" said Sophie. "To talk about Aunt Hortense?"

"Yes."

Their mother became brisk, started to clean up. She sent Paul to the garden for water. They had no running water in the house; all of it had to be carried from a tap in the garden.

Paul enjoyed going out to fetch water in the evenings in the dark. The air was so still, the countryside so peaceful. He stood for a few minutes, hearing quiet noises all around. What was that? He listened intently. Yes, he was sure it was the warbling notes of a young nightingale! About this time they began to try out their song. Their house was called "Les Rossignols". The Nightingales. They nested in the tangled undergrowth at the edge of the old damson wood beside the house. Paul was always sorry they were never here between April and June when they could hear the adult birds in full song. After the hatching of the eggs they ceased to sing.

When he came to live in the valley all year round, then he would hear the nightingales. The warble came again, a little stronger. "Thy liquid notes, that close the eye of day." He remembered his father quoting that the first night they spent in the house. He smiled to himself in the darkness, then bent to fill the bucket. He liked the idea of the nightingale closing the eye of day.

Inside the house, Mrs Grant had started to wash up, with her daughters helping.

"So I'm going off to St Girons tomorrow with Aunt Nicole."

"So soon!" said Claudine. "Aunt Nicole won't have time even to get her breath back."

"Your grandfather is worried." And that was enough.

"Mummy was lying, wasn't she?" said Sophie, when they went to bed.

"I don't know. I'm not sure," said Claudine.

She was disappointed that Aunt Nicole was going to be whisked away so quickly. She had asked her mother if she might go with them but her mother thought not, she ought to stay to help her father and to cook.

Claudine sat in front of the mirror at the little dressing-table made of orange boxes and sprigged muslin. The light was poor, she could scarcely make out her features. She leaned forward peering at her face. She was turning browner every day, she was sure she was, and when she went home everyone would envy her her tan. She fingered her chin, frowning, wondering if the blotch in the middle was going to turn into a spot. She hoped not, hated spots, always felt they were ten times bigger than they were and that everyone had their eyes on them.

"It's a wonder you don't get bored admiring yourself."

"Oh, shut up!" One of the drawbacks of holidays was having to share a room with Sophie. "I wasn't admiring myself, if you'd like to know."

"I suppose you think that German boy fancies you?"

"Don't be ridiculous!"

Claudine got up, undressed and went to bed. But when she put out the light and lay down she found that she was thinking about the boy, trying to remember what he looked like. He had been tall and rather thin with mid-brown hair. Nothing special. Nothing distinctive. Not like the house . . .

She went to sleep and dreamt of the sunflower house with its shutters wide open and them inside. Yes, it was they who were inside: she could see them sitting around a table eating and drinking. And in the room next door Paul lay awake listening for the nightingale and thinking also about the house with the garden full of sunflowers and the boy with the rug. Then he slept and dreamt also, but of his grandfather.

In the morning Claudine got up more determined than ever to try to find out about the house and its occupants. She felt that their very own house had been violated, taken over by the enemy, as it

22

were, not that she was thinking in terms of Germans being enemies, but merely the fact that strangers were occupying a place that they had always considered to belong to them.

3

The Cross-examination of Christian

THE DAY PROMISED to be hot again. It would be a good day for the laké, said their mother over breakfast. Why didn't they take a picnic? Sophie seized on the idea at once and ran off to the cowshed to pump up her bicycle tyres. Paul was agreeable enough though Claudine would have preferred to begin her investigations.

"Doing what?"

She gave him one of her withering looks which was meant to imply that he lacked imagination. That morning she, too, seemed to lack it. It must be the heat, she decided; the cool water might help clear her brain.

After the five-kilometre cycle run along the dusty rutted road they were ready to dive straight into the lake, and their parched skins received the touch of the green water gratefully.

When they came out to lie on their towels under the branches of a large spreading tree, they had a small snack. Just to keep them going, as Claudine said, distributing lumps of fresh crusty bread and slices of gleaming salami. Whilst they ate they discussed possible ways of finding out about the occupants of the sunflower house. At least Claudine and Sophie discussed tactics, making it sound like the breaking of the siege at Sebastopol; Paul lay back on his elbow half-listening, with his eyes fixed on the sky overhead. It was a deep blue. A southern blue. He wanted to find out the secret of the house too, and yet in another way did not. He felt it might not be a good idea particularly, did not quite know why; it was something that he sensed rather.

"Some things should remain mysteries," he said.

Claudine told him not to be silly, there was no point in a mystery such as that one. There was bound to be some simple explanation and there was nothing to be gained by not knowing. He did not argue, could not be bothered. It was too hot and he felt too good after his swim and with the bread and salami in his stomach.

"I could throw my ball into the garden," suggested Sophie. "And then I could go and knock at the door and ask if I could find it."

Claudine said that that was too unsubtle, something a little more sophisticated was required. Paul murmured that he didn't see why, sometimes the simplest way was the best.

"I'm good at throwing balls over garden walls," said Sophie. "I could do it so that they would think it was an accident."

Claudine did not doubt that. There was no one more devious than Sophie when she put her mind to it. And her air of innocence was definitely an asset in such ploys. Well, perhaps, said Claudine, if they couldn't think of anything else. But it would be just like the thing if the ball was to land right in the boy's lap and he threw it straight out again. They had to be sure that they got as far as the door and could look through the windows. Claudine was desperate for the sight of the inside of that house. She had thought about it for so many years, imagined what it would be like, and would never have thought of tearing the shutters away herself, but now that they were open it would be too much not to want to take a look.

Suddenly Paul said, "Speak of the devil!"

They looked round and saw, sitting no more than twenty yards away, the boy from the sunflower house.

"Looks as if you won't have to throw balls over the garden wall, at least not to get into conversation."

25

"Go and speak to him, Paul," pleaded Claudine. "Please!"

But Paul would not, said that he did not want to. He was stubborn, could not be moved; they knew that. Paul picked up his paperback book and began to read, pretending to be totally absorbed although they knew that he was not, for every now and then he turned his head slightly, as they did, to see what the boy was doing. He too was reading.

Claudine stood up, yawning. "Think I'll go and buy an ice-cream. Coming, Sophie?"

Paul groaned, put down his book to watch them go. He saw them take the route that would enable them to pass close to the German boy. Claudine stopped, affecting an air of surprise. Paul did not quite hear what she said but could well imagine. Surprise, surprise! Fancy meeting you here!

Within minutes the German boy was picking up his towel, his book, his bag, and following the girls over to the tree.

"Paul," said Claudine, "this is Christian. I've asked him to come and join us."

The boy shook hands, they all settled themselves on the grass. Sophie passed around a bag of toffees. The ice-cream appeared to have been forgotten.

Christian's English was better than his French. He commented that they seemed to speak French fluently; they told him that they were half French and so it wasn't surprising, was it?

"No," he agreed. "Not surprising."

Was he half anything? asked Sophie. No, wholly German. Was this his first visit to France? asked Claudine. Yes, he admitted, that it was. Did he like it? asked Sophie. Yes, he said that he did. That was good, said Sophie, they liked it too, very much, and she offered him another toffee which he declined, shaking his head, speaking very politely and formally. Claudine noticed that his eyes were a kind of greenish-brown; hazel would probably be the right description. He had a nice smile too, a little quick and nervous, but then he probably felt shy to be sitting with three strangers.

26

They resumed their questioning. Where was he from? Heidelberg. How nice! said Claudine. She believed that it was a lovely city although she had never been there herself. Because of their connection with France they tended to come back here year after year. They were in a rut, she supposed. Oh no, Christian objected, he did not believe that and, anyway, it must be nice to come back to a place year after year, to feel that you belonged.

"But you're not going to do that?" said Claudine. "Not here at least."

No, he agreed. Then he changed the subject, asking about Edinburgh and Scotland.

What did his father do? asked Sophie, as soon as there was a small lull, ignoring her brother and sister's frowns. That was a question you were not supposed to ask of people although she could not see why. It told you something about them, didn't it? It might not be considered rude anyway in Germany. He said that his father was a Professor of Fine Art at the University of Heidelberg.

"Snap!" said Sophie. "Ours teaches art too."

Paul explained that it was not quite the same thing: their father taught art in a large comprehensive school. Christian's father's occupation was obviously much grander. Christian laughed and said it depended on how you looked at things. He began to relax a bit now, they could see it happening.

"Perhaps our fathers should meet," suggested Claudine. "They might have a lot in common."

Christian shrugged. "My father is not very —" He could not find the word.

"Sociable?" offered Paul.

"Yes."

So the Professor of Fine Art was not sociable. He had certainly not seemed to be, calling Christian indoors when he saw him talking to the girls at the gate. And was there a mother? They did not like to ask that, even Sophie, not outright anyway.

"Our mother is a translator. She translates novels, children's books and things from English into French." She waited.

"How interesting," he said. "It must give her satisfaction."

How polite he was, thought Paul, how unlike his school friends.

"Are you an only child?" asked Sophie.

"I have one brother but he is only a half. Not a full brother, I mean! He is much older and away from home."

"So you're on your own most of the time? You're lucky."

"He is, isn't he?" said Claudine. "It must be peaceful."

She sat back and left Sophie to it. Sophie asked if he liked the house. Oh yes indeed, said Christian, he did like the house very much. It had a very nice feeling to it, the garden was good, and it was so peaceful there.

"We liked it too. Oh, not that we've ever been inside." Sophie waited. "Though we've always wanted to."

Christian said nothing. He stared out across the lake. Paul muttered something about going for another swim, it was getting hot again.

Sophie told Christian she hoped he did not mind that they had used to play in the garden. Why should he since he had not been there? he said.

"No, you weren't, were you? We wondered if you'd been hiding inside." Sophie laughed.

Christian denied it, laughing with her. Sophie's laughter was verging on the hysterical. Paul repeated again that it would be a good idea to go for a swim. His sisters did not appear even to hear.

Sophie took a deep breath. "How long have you had the house?"

Three pairs of eyes were now upon Christian. He looked puzzled for a moment, spread out his hands. Then he said, "How long? I do not know."

"You don't know," repeated Claudine and Sophie together.

"How can you not know?" asked Sophie.

He did not know why he did not know: that was clear.

"My father has it." He looked unhappy. "Not me."

"A swim," said Paul determinedly, looking at Christian, inviting him to go with him into the water. Christian said that was a

28

good idea and the boys went off, leaving the girls to buzz with speculation.

They invited the German boy to share their picnic lunch and he accepted. He said that his father had gone into Villeneuve to buy things for the house and so he was not expected back till later. All around them people were spreading picnics on the grass, and some had even brought tables and chairs with them, and table-cloths too. When it came to picnicking the French liked to do it in style. They cut up loaves of bread, set out dishes of paté, salami, cheese and salads. And there were plenty of bottles of beer and wine in evidence.

How long would he be staying? Sophie asked Christian, as she chewed her way through a thick sandwich. He thought a week perhaps, possibly more or less, depending on when they got all the things done to the house. Were they doing things? His father wanted to paint the kitchen and do a few repairs in order to sell it. The three Scottish children stopped eating. So his father did *own* the house then? Oh yes. He didn't rent it? Oh no.

Why was he selling? asked Claudine. Didn't he like it? Had he *just* bought it? Christian said that he did not know why his father was selling. He appeared not to like the house, but he appeared to have owned it for quite some time.

"No more questions," said Paul. "It's not fair on Christian. It's like the Inquisition."

"The Inquisition? You mean the Spanish Inquisition? Ah yes!" He laughed.

"They tortured people horribly at that," said Sophie, taking another slice of salami and cramming it whole into her mouth. "People are horrible when it comes to torture, the things they do, screwing their thumbs—"

"That's enough, Sophie," said Claudine. "Let's enjoy our lunch, if you don't mind."

They spent another couple of hours together after lunch, talking and swimming. They said no more about the sunflower house, talking instead of other things. Christian was interested in history and art too. He thought he might be an art historian like his father when he grew up, but he wasn't sure yet. Paul told him that he hoped to work on his grandfather's farm. And Claudine told him that she intended to go to Paris and live with her Aunt Nicole on the Left Bank.

"And you, Sophie?" Christian smiled at her.

"She's going to get a job in a Secret Intelligence Agency, cross-questioning," said Paul, and they all laughed, Sophie too. She considered there could be worse ways of earning your living.

About mid-afternoon Christian said that he must go. He became a little formal again, said that it had been a most pleasant day and he had enjoyed meeting them, very much. Claudine looked at Paul hoping that he might say that they must do this again, but Paul, as usual, and as she would have expected, said nothing of the sort. It was not easy for her – a girl – to say it, not even in this day and age, so different from their mother's, as she was so fond of telling them. Besides, Claudine was not sure how women's lib was faring in Germany. Certainly, in France, especially in the provinces, girls were not as free as they were back home, and her grandfather would have a fit if he saw her coming home unescorted through the streets in the evening. He still believed in arranged marriages!

"See you again, Christian," said Sophie. "Come and call on us. We live in the house high on the hill."

Christian nodded, said thank you, and departed. They knew he would not call.

"Odd that he knows so little about the house," said Claudine, "and how his father came about owning it."

It did seem odd that Christian should know so little, and yet they believed that that was the way it was. They knew all about what happened in their own family, how much they paid for their house and so forth. Things like that were not kept secret. But perhaps it was different in Germany. Perhaps Christian's father was an austere, formal man who thought that children should be told little. But did they know everything that happened in their own family?

They stopped to wonder, looking at one another, asking one another. They remembered *Grand-père* whispering in the house last night with their mother and father. Perhaps they did not know as much as they thought.

They stayed at the lake until hunger drew them home. As they cycled back along the road, hoses were playing on the fields watering the crops, keeping them fresh and green.

The grandparents were sitting on their verandah, still wearing their old straw hats even though they were out of the sun. The children dismounted, throwing their bicycles into the hedge and ran to see them.

But something was wrong, they could tell at once. *Grand-père* was fidgeting around, and his face looked flushed and dark. Had something happened to his sister, the one in St Girons?

"We've been at the lake," said Sophie. "There were lots of people there today."

"I know, I know," muttered the old man.

They looked at him. What did he know, what was he talking about?

Grand'mère asked them to sit down, and went to the kitchen to fetch cold drinks.

Grand-père turned to them. "I heard you were at the lake today. I heard you were talking to the German boy from the house up there." He pointed his finger angrily towards the other side of the hill.

Yes, they were, said Paul quietly, they had met him at the lake and talked to him. And they had thought that he was very nice.

"He is a German." Their grandfather's voice was rising.

"Now, now, Jean-Paul," said his wife, returning with a clinking jug of iced lemon. "Don't be getting yourself worked up."

"Worked up! Haven't I got things to be worked up about?" *Grand-père* was getting more and more excited. He was a very emotional man, much more so than their grandfather back in Edinburgh who was an accountant, level-headed, and believed strongly in self-control.

Grand'mère poured the cold drinks into glasses and handed them to the children. *Grand-père* muttered on under his breath. It was terribly boring, thought Claudine, that he had to go on and on hating Germans, all Germans. They were not asking him to accept the ones that he had fought against or the ones who had executed his brother. But a German boy of fifteen like Christian, what could be wrong with him?

"I do not want you to talk to that boy again," said *Grand-père* abruptly. "I do not want it."

"But, *Grand-père*," protested Claudine, "that's silly—"

"It is not silly," he shouted, colour mounting in his face bringing red to the surface of the wrinkled brown skin. "I will not have you associating with Germans. I will not!"

Claudine pointed out that they were not associating with Germans, only one, and he was of their own age.

"You can't possibly have anything against him, *Grand-père*, can you?"

Grand-père would not say whether he could or not; he repeated again that he did not want them to talk to him, to be friends with him. He said that they should do as he wished. He was their grandfather, was he not, and they should respect his wishes?

Their grandmother sighed. She said that it was difficult for the children to understand, but he cut in saying that it did not matter if they understood or not, they must do as he wished. And then he got up and disappeared into the house, swishing aside the ribboned curtain that hung over the doorway.

"You must try to understand," said their grandmother. "And you must try not to upset him. He is an old man and his blood pressure is high. It's not good for him to get excited."

They pushed their bicycles up the drive to the house. Sophie said that she thought their grandfather was a silly old man.

"Don't speak that way about him," said Paul sharply. "You don't know what he's been through."

They didn't have to go over all *that* again, said Claudine.

"Christian wasn't in the war, was he?" said Sophie.

"Precisely," said Claudine.

Whether it was reasonable of *Grand-père* or not was beside the question, said Paul: they would have to make sure that they did not upset him. They would have to be careful, they did not want to make him ill, and that might mean boycotting Christian and the sunflower house.

4

Consternation at the Café de Commerce

THE GRANTS ATE out that evening, at the *Café de Commerce* in a small town a few miles away. They often went there and the proprietor and his wife knew them well.

Madame ushered them now into the long narrow dining-room at the back of the building overlooking the river. She had the best table in the room for them, their usual one, by the window, where they could look down on the slow-moving water below. She talked to them as she led them to the table, saying how nice it was to see them back again and how quickly the year had slipped past! So preoccupied were they with her and with settling at their table that it was not until they had sat down that they realised that Christian and his father were sitting in the corner.

Sophie noticed them first. Of course. It so happened that she had the seat facing the corner. She kicked Claudine under the table and pointed. Claudine turned swiftly to look and then nudged Paul. Christian bowed, just a little, inclining his head forward over the red and white checked tablecloth. His father had stopped eating, had laid down his knife and fork and was staring ahead. Then, hurriedly, meeting Paul's eye, he resumed eating, gazing downwards.

"Well, what have you on this evening, Madame Roget?" asked Mrs Grant.

Madame Roget reeled off a list of mouth-watering dishes. The

34

children did not hear a word, had to have them all repeated, making their mother tut with irritation.

They ordered. Mr Grant poured some wine from the litre bottle standing on the table. He and his wife leant back comfortably, in a mood of contentment, and contemplated the view across the river. Claudine and Paul sat rigid, wishing that they could turn their heads again. Only Sophie could gaze serenely and innocently straight ahead, which she did, relentlessly.

Christian's father was very much an older version of Christian: tall, lean, mid-brown hair. He looked rather distinguished, thought Claudine, just what she would have expected a Professor of Fine Art to look like, if she had ever given the matter any thought. She decided that Christian himself was more distinctive than she had thought at first sight; he had the kind of face that grew on you and you found yourself remembering. She stole another glimpse, after manoeuvring the dropping of her serviette. From half under the table she observed that the professor was scrutinizing them, and he was frowning and not eating any more. Christian had an embarrassed, and somewhat bewildered, air.

Madame Roget brought the *hors d'oeuvre*, which looked like a full meal in itself.

"This should fill a corner or two, eh?" said their father.

He noticed that his three children were less eager than usual to start eating and appeared to be more interested in something in the corner of the room. He looked to see what it was but seemed not to find anything interesting there himself. There had been no flash of recognition, realised Claudine, who had been monitoring his reaction.

"I'm hungry at any rate," said their mother. And then she too glanced idly at the corner to see what it was that was distracting them. She dropped the spoon on top of the tomatoes. It fell with a clang against the edge of the china plate, bounced off the table and struck the floor. It was really only a small noise but it might have been the clanging of a fire bell for it raised all heads in the dining room. And then, as she bent to retrieve it, she knocked her wineglass sideways, sending a streak of red across the checked cloth.

Her face had changed completely: it was no longer relaxed and gay, but shocked and pale, as if she had seen a ghost. And the professor was staring at her with the same kind of expression. Mr Grant coughed, breaking the spell, and made some remark about messing up Madame's clean cloth.

"What? Oh yes." Mrs Grant began to dab at the stain with her serviette. The she helped herself to the *hors d'oeuvre* with an air of abstraction, as if she did not really see what it was she was putting on her plate. Her hand was still none too steady. Mr Grant talked, telling them that he intended to start landscaping the garden next day.

Claudine could not keep her mind on the food or the garden. Her head was whirling.

"Come on, Claudine," said her father. "It's not like you, you're usually starving."

They finished the *hors d'oeuvre*. Madame Roget brought the meat. Christian and his father were having their dessert.

"No coffee, thank you," they heard the professor say. "May we have our bill please?" He spoke French well.

Mr Grant talked on, aided by Sophie who could talk under any conditions. And every now and then she smiled in Christian's direction. Christian smiled back, but bleakly. He looks surprised, thought Paul, as if he does not quite know what is happening. As they did not.

"Chicken's delicious," said Mr Grant. "No one is as good with sauces as Madame Roget. Isn't that right, Françoise?"

"Oh yes. Or no – I mean –" She lifted up her knife and fork again but only picked at the food, and when Madame Roget came to clear the dishes she chided her. Mrs Grant pleaded a slight headache. She thought she was just a little off colour; it was the heat, you know, and she was not used to it yet. Not after the cooler climate of Scotland. Madame Roget nodded, saying that she had heard how cold and wet it was from Mrs Grant's mother. Ah yes, they were sorry for Mrs Grant having to live in that nasty grey climate.

Christian and his father were making a move. Their chairs scraped as they were pushed back from the table. The professor walked past, head, shoulders, back erect, but just as they were about to leave the room Christian swivelled round briefly and engaged Paul's eye.

It was as if a weight had been lifted from their heads: tension had gone from the room. Mrs Grant drank a glass of wine and ate her dessert. She began to talk and laugh again, though a hint of anxiety remained in her eyes.

It was late by the time they returned home and the children went straight to bed. There was little chance for them to discuss the happening in the restaurant, except for a few whispers exchanged by the girls. Claudine lay awake for a long time, her head spinning with fantastic thoughts. And when she slept she dreamt of her mother and the German Professor of Fine Art.

In the morning, after breakfast, they set off for a walk.

"I've been thinking," said Claudine.

"I'll bet!" Paul plucked a long grass from the edge of the road and twisted it round his hand until it almost cut into the skin. He was not sure that he wanted to think. He wished again that his sisters could let things lie. What was the point in poking and prying?

"I think Mummy must have been in love with the professor," declared Sophie, giving a little skip of excitement.

"So do I," said Claudine. "There can be no other solution."

Paul pointed out that there could be dozens of solutions, it was ridiculous to jump to such a conclusion so quickly. The fact that their mother had recognised the professor did not prove that she had ever been in love with him. How silly they were! Paul threw the grass away. In the field on the left-hand side the farmer was cutting his hay and stacking it up. Paul resolved to go and help his grandfather that morning. He felt like some hard outdoor work, involving the land, and having the wide sky overhead and neither of his sisters chattering beside him. His grandfather did not talk all that much; he spoke sporadically but when he did he usually had something definite to say. Not like all this silly tittle-tattle! Really, girls *were* bad that way, whatever they said. Boys didn't waste their time on it.

"Don't tell me you're not interested," said Claudine. "I know you, Paul Grant. You like to pretend it's beneath your notice but I usually see your ears flapping."

Paul lunged for her but she ducked and ran up the road laughing. Dancing backwards, she taunted him, telling him how pure he was, how sensible! A paragon of virtue. On the bend she almost fell over Christian.

The German boy caught hold of her, steadying her by the elbows. Then he said very politely, "*Bonjour*."

Claudine recovered her balance and composure and returned the greeting. She was delighted to see him. It was a bit of luck really, for perhaps they could discuss with him what had happened in the café and see what he had made of it. But Christian looked uncommunicative, as if he had retreated into himself and was wearing a shell of polite armour.

"Are you going to the lake today?" asked Sophie.

No, Christian did not think so.

"Pity," said Sophie. "We were hoping you would be there. Claudine said so just this morning."

Claudine glared at her sister and itched to kick her in the shins. Christian said that he would be busy that day, they had much work to do in the house. He did not speak in the friendly open way of the day before and even as he spoke his eyes were scanning the road that led to his house. Perhaps his father had a pair of binoculars and was spying on them, thought Claudine. It seemed ridiculous but the whole business had an air of absurdity to it.

"I must leave now," he said.

The three Scottish children were blocking the road. Only Paul moved aside.

"Will you come to the lake tomorrow, Christian?" asked Sophie. "Please!"

"I would like to but –" Christian broke off and shrugged.

"Why can't you then?"

Christian said again that they had a lot of work to do in the house which most probably was true but sounded more like an excuse than a reason. Sophie told him that she thought he ought to try to come, it wasn't good for anyone to work too hard in this heat, and wasn't the lake lovely?

"Stop pestering, Sophie," said Paul. "Christian knows where the lake is and he can come if he wants to."

"I would like to see you," said the German boy hesitantly. "It is not that I would not –"

Claudine decided to be bold. After all, why not? There was nothing to be lost. She said, "Doesn't your father want you to see us?"

Christian's face flushed. He began to protest, then nodded. "I do not understand . . . He will not explain. He is not usually an unreasonable man and I am confused."

"We are too."

"Your mother and father do not want you to see me?"

It was their grandfather, explained Sophie, who *hated* Germans. Paul jumped in quickly to explain about his grandfather fighting with the Resistance and of course such people had very bitter memories. He expected that Christian's father might have had them too against the French and British.

"Was your father in the war?" asked Claudine.

"Yes. He was about twenty when the war ended, I believe."

Claudine grew excited. "Was he in France, do you know?"

Christian shook his head. He said that his father had fought on the Russian Front and been taken prisoner by the Russians. He had had some unpleasant experiences there.

"So I expect he is not too fond of Russians then?" said Paul.

"He never speaks much about it. He is a kind man, not resentful, no, not at all. That is why I do not understand." And Christian looked unhappy again.

They could not stand there on the road too long since either

Christian's father or their grandfather might come by. Paul thought for a moment and then suggested that they all meet at a stretch of river further along the valley in the afternoon. When they didn't want to go as far as the lake they often went to the river to swim. There was never anyone else there but themselves and the birds. Christian said that that was a very good idea, he would like to come, and so they arranged to meet at three o'clock. Paul took a stick and drew a map in the dust on the road. He would find it, said Christian. Then he said goodbye and left them quickly, walking fast, to return to the sunflower house and his father.

"Interesting," said Claudine. "But it doesn't quite make sense yet. I thought his father must have been here in the war with the Occupation Forces and that would be how he had met *Grand-père*."

"If he had been then he couldn't have had anything to do with Mother, stupid!" said Paul. "Mother was about ten when the war ended."

They walked slowly back along the road, heads bent, even Sophie's, for she too was deep in thought. Christian's father must have bought the house after the war and come to live there and met their mother then, suggested Claudine. That must be it!

"They fell in love and *Grand-père* wouldn't let Mother marry him. So he went away heartbroken and Mother went to Edinburgh and married Father."

"I don't like that story much," said Sophie.

No, neither did Paul, though he did not say so, for it implied that their mother had only taken their father at second best. Second best to the professor! Claudine told Sophie that she was just a silly little romantic girl, that it was a mistake to think that people only fell in love once in their lives. She intended to fall in love many times herself before she married. How would you know if you had chosen the right man or not if you hadn't been in love with others before?

Paul said that it must have happened a long time ago, so it was odd that their mother should be so disturbed. She should have got over him by now after all! What if she had not? Claudine

40

wondered uneasily if perhaps her mother might fall in love with the professor all over again. Surely not. Not at her age! But then she thought of a friend of her mother's back home in Edinburgh who had just got married in the spring and *seemed* to be in love with the man, a fat balding widower with five children.

Paul left them at his grandfather's farm, saying that he would see them at lunch-time. The girls continued up the hill to "Les Rossignols". There were voices on the verandah, fast voices, talking and talking and talking. Aunt Nicole must have arrived! She had. She came forward to greet them, kissing them on both cheeks, exclaiming how much they had grown and how lovely it was to see them. She smelled of expensive scent and was dressed in an ice-blue linen dress. They settled on the terrace to have a long chat.

"I am so annoyed," declared Aunt Nicole. "Your mother and I have to go to the Pyrenees *today*. Imagine! And I have just arrived! I was looking forward so much to the peace and quiet." She shrugged, making the bracelets on her slim wrists jingle. Claudine eyed her own wrists and saw that they were thicker than Aunt Nicole's *already*. She sighed.

Mrs Grant said that there was no question but that they would have to go; their father was very concerned about his sister and they all knew the strong bond that existed between them, even though they had not met for many years.

"I know, I know! Still, I have a whole month so I suppose I shouldn't complain." But Aunt Nicole was tired after the long hot weeks she had just worked through in the city. She told them about the luxurious apartments she had been refurbishing on one of the big boulevards. She described the materials and colours, making it all sound very exciting. Claudine wondered if she too should become an interior designer, but she was not too fond of Doing-it-Yourself and sewing up curtains, which was how Aunt Nicole had begun. She had slowly but gradually built up a very good business and was now able to live well, without having to do any manual work herself any more.

An hour or so later their mother and aunt put a few things into the back of the latter's car and drove off south towards the high Pyrenees. The children went to meet Christian.

5

House to House Enquiries à la Claudine

CHRISTIAN WAS WAITING for them at the river. He sat on the bank with his jeans rolled up above his knees, his long narrow feet swaying to and fro in the cool, clear water.

"The water is lovely. So cool, so refreshing. I like it better than the lake. No other peoples!"

The water was only thigh deep here, but even so they could swim a little and splash about. Trees hung over the river on this stretch, giving shade, making the light golden-green.

"I like this region very much." Christian sighed. "I would like very much if my father would keep the house."

Why didn't he? asked Sophie. He shrugged. How long had his father had the house? asked Claudine. Had he been able to find out? He said that he had asked and his father had been very off-hand, saying that he had acquired it at some point.

"At some point?" said Sophie. "What does that mean?"

"It's just the kind of phrase parents use when they want to put you off," said Claudine.

"But why should my father want to?"

Claudine hugged her knees up to her chin. "You see, Christian, there is some mystery about your family and ours. Concerning your house."

Christian's brow was drawn together and his hazel-coloured

43

eyes looked a little pained. He could not understand why there should be any such mystery. His father was not a mysterious man, he said, shaking his head. Reserved, yes; mysterious, no.

"It is always the people who seem least mysterious who have the most mysteries," said Claudine.

Paul laughed. "Words of wisdom! You sound like an oracle pronouncing."

Claudine did not deign to answer. She hoped that Christian's limited knowledge of the English language prevented him from understanding some of the nastier digs inflicted by her brother and sister. "But there *is* some mystery. And I for one am determined to find out what. I intend to make systematic enquiries."

"What kind of enquiries are these?" asked Christian.

"It's the way the police talk," said Paul.

"Police?"

"We are not going to the police, Christian," said Claudine. "Paul, you are just confusing the issue, and Christian."

She had been thinking, she said, and had decided that the only way to find out anything was from the locals. She intended to go from house to house.

"You're caught up in the old police jargon again," said Paul. "House to house enquiries!"

Claudine ignored him. She would not ask direct questions of course, certainly not: that would be too unsubtle and would yield no results. In the past they had often tried it to find out about the house and found that people clammed up immediately it was mentioned. They shrugged and pretended to know nothing. And they themselves had not pressed their questions home, being content enough to let the house have a secret, since it was shuttered and abandoned anyway. But now that it was opened up, now that something was known about it, all must be known. At least, so said Claudine. Paul himself said nothing. He was watching a kingfisher further down the river: it was perched on a low branch hanging over the water. He would not be able to get between Claudine and a notion anyway, that he had learned a long time ago.

44

During the course of the afternoon, between bouts of splashing and playing in the water, they learned a little more about Christian. His mother had died two years ago, after several years of being an invalid. His father's life had not been an easy one, with a sick wife to care for. His brother was a student and engaged to be married. Christian and his father lived a fairly quiet life now. "My father has a few good close friends but he is not a party man."

"I can believe that," said Claudine. "I mean to say, he didn't look particularly . . ." She let the sentence trail away, not wishing to say anything against Christian's father, and anyway the afternoon was hot and the insects were buzzing thickly around making a steady droning noise. She felt her eyelids drooping. She lay back in the grass letting her head rest on a clump of cornflowers and for a little while dozed and forgot to question Christian.

When the sun was dipping westward, Christian said that he must be off.

"Shall we see you tomorrow?" said Claudine.

He nodded. Same time, same place! He took his leave of them and went ahead, leaving them to wait a few minutes before they too emerged on the road. The road, baking in the late afternoon sunshine, dazzled their eyes for a few minutes after their thick green retreat.

"He's nice," said Sophie. "I like him."

"Not easy to get to know though," said Paul. "He is reserved."

Who wouldn't be? Claudine wanted to know, shut up in an apartment in Heidelberg with a father who was a Professor of Fine Art and didn't like parties. In their house in Edinburgh people were always coming and going, drinking cups of tea and coffee and glasses of wine, talking late into the night. Christian would have none of that in his life. He must be very lonely.

"Not necessarily," said Paul. "He might like it. Times I wouldn't mind a bit of loneliness myself." Claudine informed him that he wouldn't like it if he had it. "Try me!" He gazed out over the fields at his grandfather's farm and knew that he wouldn't be lonely when he came to live here, parties or no parties.

Claudine announced that she intended to begin her systematic enquiries that very moment. "See you later!" She left them abruptly. She wanted to go alone, without Paul to give warning looks and without Sophie who never knew when to stop. She turned off up the driveway that led to the Leclercs' farm.

Old Madame Leclerc, the grandmother, was seated on the verandah keeping an eye on the chickens and young children. She was aged, had always seemed so to the Grant children even when they were small, and her main function in life was to sit on the verandah and keep an eye open for disasters. She wore a rusty-looking black dress and a battered straw bonnet. She looked up as Claudine approached and for a moment did not recognise her. And then Claudine spoke, wishing her good day.

"Ach, Claudine!" Madame Leclerc spoke with a thick harsh accent which Claudine had to listen to carefully.

The girl stepped up on to the verandah observing that it was hot. Madame agreed that yes, it was hot. She only had four brown teeth that clinked together when she spoke. The Widow Leclerc: that was how she was known in the district. She lived with her son and daughter-in-law and their children. The French were good that way, thought Claudine; they didn't put their old out to languish in a home. For a moment or two she chatted to the old woman about the weather, this year's plum crop and the grandchildren. And then she began on the first leg of her systematic enquiries.

"You know the house half-way up the hill before you come to the church?" Did Madame Leclerc know the one she was speaking of? But the widow appeared not to. Their house? No, no, said Claudine, endeavouring to be patient; the one on the other side of the valley. "Mon Repos" she believed it was called; its name was just visible in weathered letters on the gate. She hated the name and they never used it themselves. The old woman repeated it. Then she shook her head. She never went out these days, her arthritis was bad and she couldn't get as far as the gate unless her son took her in his car. What it was to be old! Did Claudine realise how lucky she was to be young and agile? She liked to go to market in Villeneuve now and then but even that was crowded and full of strange faces. Now in the old days. . . .

Claudine excused herself at the first opportunity and went to the door of the house, calling out to the younger Madame Leclerc.

"*Entrez!*" Madame Leclerc called from the cool depths of the house.

Claudine found her in the kitchen ironing clothes. She was a plump, cheerful woman, always pleased to see the Grants.

Claudine began again on the weather and the plum crop, asked about the children, and then mentioned the house again. Madame Leclerc put down her iron with a smack.

"Why are you interested in that house, Claudine?"

"We've met the boy of the house."

"Oh yes, I heard that there was someone in there now." Madame Leclerc took a sheet, folded it and hung it on a clothes horse. Her lips were pursed. She knew nothing whatsoever about the house. It had been shut up when she came to the valley as a bride twelve years before. And she had understood then that the house had already been shut up for years. Sometimes, when the first child was born, she used to walk up that way with him in the pram, but now that she had several children she had no time to take walks.

"So you don't know anything about the house?" said Claudine.

"Nothing at all."

"Your husband might?"

Well, he might, Madame Leclerc agreed, but she could not say. They had never discussed it. Why should they? It was only an empty house with an overgrown garden and they had other things to attend to. She slapped another sheet on to the ironing board. Claudine had never seen her idle, even on the hottest, heaviest day of summer.

She left the house, going slowly along the road, watching for a sight of Monsieur Leclerc in the fields. She saw him in his blue overalls in a field of tomatoes. She went to him, commenting on the delicious smell of the plants. He shook hands with her, asked

47

how they all were in turn.

"Monsieur Leclerc, you know the house half-way up the hill towards the church?"

She was watching him carefully to see if he would react and was certain that he did. His eyes changed, ceased to focus on her and looked a little to one side. He shrugged (oh, that maddening shrug!), saying that the house had been empty a long long time. And now he must be about his work, he had a lot to do, the tomatoes were ripening fast and his stomach was beginning to feel pangs of hunger. He slapped his stomach and laughed.

"Are you sure you know nothing?" Claudine was beginning to feel desperate. She felt as if she was trying to plough through a sea of cotton-wool. There seemed to her to be only what she could term a conspiracy of silence. Someone *must* know something. Not all that many people lived in the valley, and most of them had been born and bred here, so surely they would know who the owner of the house was.

"I know nothing, Claudine. Except that my tomatoes ripen fast."

She left him to his tomatoes. Before she went, he put a fat one into her hand. They were different from the ones at home, being much larger and juicier, and tasting ten times better.

Munching on her gift, she continued along the road. Whom should she question now? She must make some progress this afternoon so that she would go back with something to report. She flapped a fly from her face. She was beginning to feel very irritated indeed. The road was empty, and there was only her grandparents' farm ahead.

And then she thought of Madame Grenier. Madame Grenier was the nearest neighbour of the sunflower house, excepting the presbytery, which no longer had a resident priest but had been renovated and was used as a holiday house by some people from Paris. She could go to Madame Grenier's house by the back way, need not pass near Christian and his father.

She climbed the hill, found Madame Grenier and her husband at home in their little, dilapidated cottage in need of repairs that it would never get, not as long as *they* lived.

They greeted her warmly, set her down on a dusty chair to sip a little prune liqueur. It was very dim inside, with the shutters half-closed, and she could scarcely make out the two old people. She would certainly not be able to read their expressions.

She brought the conversation round to the house.

"Unlucky house that!" said Monsieur. "Not good."

Madame tetched, got up and clucked around the room, a bit, thought Claudine, like one of her own hens which ran freely all over the ground outside. "Marcel," she cried. "Marcel! *Assez! Assez!* Enough," she shouted several times but he did not hear, he was very deaf. He said again that the house was unlucky and no one would ever want to live in it, unless some strangers bought it who did not know its past.

"Marcel!" She was at his ear now. "You say no more. *Rien du tout!*" Her hands were working like scissors cutting the air.

"Eh?" He cupped his ear. All of a sudden he seemed to catch on to her confusion. He peered at Claudine. "Ah, yes. Yes . . . Well." He mumbled, and fumbled for his pipe and tobacco, spilling shreds of the flake down his stained corduroy trousers.

That was the end of the conversation.

Claudine returned home to announce that she had drawn a total blank, except that Monsieur Grenier thought the house was unlucky and his wife had got excited when he said so. Paul said that he was not a bit surprised she had learned nothing for he doubted if there was much to learn. Perhaps many years ago the professor had come here and their grandfather had been rude to him. And frightened him away just like that, like Miss Muffet scared by a spider? said Claudine scornfully. Did Paul think that such a man as the professor could be frightened off so easily, so that he had not dared to come back for twenty years?

The following morning she took out her bicycle and cycled to the village four kilometres further up the valley.

At the *boulangerie*, whilst she bought two long sticks of bread, she asked casually if they had seen the Germans who had come to stay in the valley. Yes, the woman had, though knew nothing about them or their house. At the *tabac*, whilst buying postcards and stamps, Claudine asked again. The response was the same, and at the *boucherie*. She thought that the woman at the butcher's clammed up in the way that the Leclercs had done. She became brisk and slapped the meat on the counter, reminding Claudine of the way that Madame Leclerc had slapped the sheet on the ironing board.

There was one other shop to try, a sort of general store-cum-haberdashers, full of old-fashioned goods that looked as if they had been left over from the war. It was owned by a little old woman with a bent back and wispy white hair.

Claudine went in and bought a length of green ribbon to tie back her own hair which was very long and hot in this weather.

Oh yes, Madame knew that house! It had been empty for years. Did she remember it when people lived in it? asked Claudine, hardly daring to move a fraction, watching the door in case some-one would come in and disturb them. The old woman raked her memory. There had been a family, four or five children, and a grandfather, she believed. What was their name now? Gaillard! She came out with it triumphantly. And after them? Did they move? They went to Marseilles, she believed, and then a man bought the house.

"A man?" Claudine felt excitement gather in her. "Was he German, Madame?"

"Yes, he was German." Suddenly, the old woman peered across the counter at Claudine. "You are the grand-daughter of the Vidals, are you not?"

"I am. But the house, Madame –"

"Why do you, the grand-daughter of the Vidals, come here asking me questions about *that* house?"

"It's just that I have often wondered about it."

"You should not wonder then." She began to mutter, to rake amongst cards of elastic with her gnarled fingers. "It will do you

50

no good."

Claudine tied her hair back firmly. When she said goodbye, the old woman did not even lift her head; she was still muttering.

"Une tragédie. Une vraie tragédie."

Was that what it was that she was saying?

6

Snakes, Sunflowers and the Professor

"SOMETHING BAD *must* have happened in that house," said Claudine. She turned to Christian. "Your house."

"What kind of bad thing?" Sophie's eyes were large.

They were back beside the river again, at their own spot. Claudine paused to watch a brown and orange butterfly flit over her head before she spoke again. The butterflies were marvellous here.

"A crime perhaps."

"A crime!" said Sophie.

Paul was investigating something moving in the long grass, pretending that he was not listening, but the girls knew that he was. Christian's eyes were on Claudine, and he was frowning.

"A *crime passionel*. Well, it could be, couldn't it?" Claudine went on defiantly, addressing her brother who was now looking at her sceptically. The trouble with Paul, she considered, was that he had his feet too firmly planted on the earth and was inclined to dismiss anything unproven as impossible.

What kind of *crime passionel*? Sophie wanted to know.

Claudine eyed Christian. "We think that perhaps your father and our mother . . ."

"My father and your mother?"

"We think they might have been in love sometime." Claudine felt herself blush.

"But how could that be?" said Christian.

It was only one of Claudine's silly theories, Paul put in quickly: she had no evidence whatsoever to support it. Claudine denied this hotly, saying that there was some evidence.

"Slender."

"It's more a feeling I have."

"Feminine intuition!"

"But if there was a *crime passionel*, as you call it," said Christian slowly, "who was the victim? Who was killed? There has to be a victim. No?"

"Not necessarily. Obviously nobody was killed. At least, how do we know?"

Paul said she should leave it, it was getting ridiculous. There was probably very little to it at all. She had a suspicious mind, that was all. He got up and said that he was going into the river. Sophie went with him, squealing and splashing, leaving Claudine and Christian on the bank. Christian was still frowning.

"My father is unusual at the moment. Not as normal. He puzzles me."

"In what way?"

"He told me to stay away from you three. That is not like him. When I asked him why he did not answer properly. He said something about there being no point to it. Since we would be leaving."

"That was not a good enough reason, was it?"

Paul and Sophie returned, dripping wet, splashing them with water that felt like drops of ice against their hot skins.

"Christian, perhaps your father and our grandfather fought a duel," said Claudine.

He said that he did not think so, his father was peaceable and had never fought a duel in his life, was against such things as that. It was a mad idea.

"She is mad," said Paul.

Claudine's temper flared. "No wonder, with a brother like you to put up with!" She looked back at Christian. "But don't

53

Germans fight duels quite a lot?"

And then she stopped, realising how silly it was to lump all Germans into anything. Their father was always checking them for that. The French do this, the Scots do that. You must always speak of individual people, he said.

"You are thinking of times past," said Christian. "Few modern Germans fight duels."

"We used to draw and quarter people in our country," said Paul. "We were very barbaric."

Claudine ignored him. She asked Christian if he had got any more information about the house from his father. He said that he had tried but his father did not want to talk of it. He said that he had only come back here to sell.

Back? Claudine pounced on the word at once. Had he really said that? Christian thought so. Yes, he was sure that his father had. So that proved then that he had been here before! declared Claudine. He must have been the German occupant who followed the Gaillards.

Paul caught her by the arms and hauled her into the river, ignoring her shrieks of protest. Submersion in water would do her good, he informed her, calm her down a bit.

Later in the afternoon the boys decided to go fishing. Paul went off up to the house to fetch two fishing rods, leaving Christian with his sisters by the river.

"And you are not to ask him any questions while I'm away!"

Claudine lay back on the grass with her arms behind her head pillowing it, staring through the gently moving green leaves at the blue sky. A plan was forming in her head.

When Paul returned with the rods she said that she and Sophie would leave them to it, they were not interested in fishing and Sophie would probably only disturb the fish since she could not sit still or keep quiet for more than five minutes at a time, if that. The boys were going to wade further downstream anyway.

"Come on, small sister!"

Sophie came away with Claudine, protesting that she would

54

have liked to have stayed. She liked the river. Claudine informed her that she had other plans for them whilst the boys were busy. They would go up to the house first, she was going to start dinner, and Sophie was going to fetch her ball!

Their father was lying on the terrace sleeping, an open book beside him. His feet were burnt a fiery red. They wakened him and he sat up rubbing his eyes and yelping when he felt his feet. He hobbled inside looking for cold cream.

Claudine buttered a chicken, wrapped it in tinfoil and put it into the oven. Then she told Sophie to bring the ball and come with her.

They took the road on the other side of the valley and went up the hill to the church. Claudine gave Sophie her instructions. The affair must be handled carefully and Sophie must not say too much or ask too many direct questions. The professor looked like a man who could easily be one step ahead of them. He was no easy game, like some of the women who served in the shops and did not realize they were being quizzed.

Just before they came to the sunflower house they stopped and Sophie began to bounce her ball up and down in the road. As she bounced her ball she sang a song, "One, two, three a-leerie, four, five, six a-leerie . . ." Claudine tried to squint through the hedge but could see nothing but blurs of yellow.

"Now!" she whispered.

Sophie lobbed the ball up and over the high hedge out of sight, into the garden. At once Claudine hastened to the gate, saying as she went, "Oh dear, Sophie, what a nuisance you are! I'll have to go and ask if you can get it back."

It was essential to get the gate open and be in the garden before the professor could retrieve the ball and throw it out. As she stepped down the two steps into the garden she saw that the professor himself was sitting in a corner in a deck-chair with a book between his hands. He was looking at her.

"*Bonjour*," she said, feeling suddenly nervous. He had such a steady, level gaze that it made her feel he could see right through into the middle of her head.

"*Bonjour*," he returned, rising to his feet and laying his book down in his deck chair. He inclined his head slightly towards her. He added in good English, "You are looking for your ball?"

"Yes, we are. Sophie here – my little sister – was bouncing it too hard and it went right over the hedge." Claudine spoke rapidly. "May we go and look for it please?"

"By all means." The same incline of the head, the same politeness. He seemed to be able to speak English much better than his son. Well, of course that was only to be expected. After all, he did have a few years' start on Christian. How old was the professor anyway? Claudine wondered, as she set to work amongst the sunflowers with Sophie panting behind her. She found it difficult to guess grown-ups' ages but thought the professor must be at least ten years older than their mother. That probably didn't matter. They could still have been in love.

"Can I help you?" he asked behind her. She thanked him politely but said that he should not trouble himself. She was sure they could find it themselves. She had instructed Sophie that they must not find it too soon, if at all. As long as possible must be spent in the sunflower garden.

Claudine straightened herself and shook back her hair which was still damp from the river. She could smell a faint, weedy smell coming from it. "The sunflowers are high, aren't they?" She smiled at him.

"They are indeed. Very high. I like tall sunflowers, do you?" Claudine said that she did.

Did she know that the Incas of Peru had used them in their religious ceremonies? "They worshipped the God of Day, you see. And the virgins in the Temple of the Sun were crowned with sunflowers."

"That must have looked nice," said Sophie, fancying herself crowned with sunflowers. She must try it, except that their stems were so tough they were terribly difficult to pick.

Did he know the story about Clytie the water-nymph who was

so saddened by the treachery of her lover Apollo that she pined away and was changed into a sunflower? countered Claudine. He nodded.

"Perhaps your garden's full of sad water-nymphs," suggested Sophie.

He said gravely that he hoped not. He did not like that idea.

"It's a lovely garden," said Claudine. "And a lovely house."

"Yes, it is beautiful here." The professor spoke now with an air of abstraction, as though he had almost forgotten that they were there.

"It's a pity you have to leave then."

"Yes." The word was clipped, as if it was intended to be final.

Claudine resumed searching, saw the ball lying at the foot of a sunflower, passed it by, tugging Sophie after her. The professor had not gone back to his chair but had remained standing in the middle of the garden gazing out towards the road. He had a very finely made face, thought Claudine, delicate-looking almost, for a man. He and Christian were very alike.

The girls worked their way through the garden. Claudine chided Sophie softly for being such a duffer. Look at the nuisance they were being to the professor!

Suddenly, Sophie, shrieking wildly, leapt up into the air and came back down again half knocking her sister over. They staggered amongst the flowers, flattening some and clutching at one another for balance.

"What on earth . . .?"

"A snake! A snake!"

"Come out at once," said the professor urgently. He held out his hands.

They took them, one each, and he pulled them clear of the sunflowers.

"Are you bitten?" Anxiously, he knelt down in front of Sophie to examine her legs. They were brown, scratched and insect-bitten.

She shook her head. She trembled.

"Are you sure you saw one, Sophie?" asked Claudine.

"Yes. It slid over my foot. It was the same one!"

"The same one?" said the professor.

"She saw a snake up at our house a few days ago. It was brown and yellow. Striped."

"So was this one." Sophie was recovering, beginning now to enjoy being at the centre of the drama. "It was gi-normous." She held her hands very wide apart.

"Gi-normous? What is that?"

"A mixture of gigantic and enormous," explained Claudine.

He nodded.

"I know it was the same snake," said Sophie. "I recognised it."

"You couldn't have." Claudine appealed to Christian's father. "Could she?"

"I am not too well acquainted with snakes, I am glad to say. I suppose it is possible it was the same snake."

"Could it come down the hill and up the hill?"

"I would imagine so. But it does not really matter, does it – where it came from?"

No, Claudine agreed, though it would be interesting to *know*. He smiled. It would be interesting to know all sorts of things that one could never know for sure, he said. He told them to sit down whilst he got a broom and had a look in the sunflowers to see if the snake was still there.

"Be careful," warned Sophie. "You might get bit."

He promised to be very careful. He fetched a broom and poked the end of it amongst the tall flowers. He did not uncover the snake.

"Slippery creatures they are, eh?"

Sophie shuddered.

"They do not harm you if you do not disturb them." He laid the broom aside. But he had sighted the ball. He stopped and retrieved it. "Catch!" He held it up in his right hand, then tossed it to Sophie, who caught it neatly against her chest.

"Thank you." Sophie smiled sweetly up at him.

"Are you staying for the summer?" he asked. He seemed to want to talk now.

Claudine launched into a description of how they came every summer and how they had bought their house up on the hill three years ago. She told him about their grandparents having the farm, although she suspected that he already knew that. And he listened, nodding from time to time, as if he wanted her to go on.

"Can I offer you a drink? Some lemonade? It is a very hot afternoon and you have had a disturbing experience."

"That would be lovely," said Claudine. They followed him into the house. They were in, at last!

It was cool inside, and dim after the bright light out of doors. For a moment they could not see clearly. He took them to the kitchen, a long, low room at the back, with a stone-flagged floor and a window looking out on to the garden behind. It had been freshly white-washed and was clean and pleasant. There were flowers, picked from the garden, though no sunflowers, in almond-green pottery vases. The house had no air of a crime having been committed in it. It had an agreeable, serene feeling to it, as if you could settle in and begin living without any more ado. Claudine felt confused.

A well-known reproduction of a painting of sunflowers was pinned to the pine dresser. She went up close to look at it.

"Van Gogh," said the professor.

She nodded. "Yes, I know. He went to live in Provence and he cut off his ear, didn't he?"

"Horrible." Sophie shivered, putting a hand up to feel that her ear was still there.

"He had a difficult temperament," said the professor. "But he was a very fine painter."

"I suppose you like painting a lot," said Sophie, "seeing as you're a professor of it?" She went on to tell him about their father. "It's a pity you two can't meet and talk about it."

"Yes, it is," he said gravely. "I know your name is Sophie, but I don't believe I know yours?"

"Claudine."

"And I am Otto Brander." He drew out two seats. "Would you like to sit down, Sophie and Claudine?"

They sat by the scrubbed wooden kitchen table and he took a jug of lemon juice from the fridge. He poured himself a glass too, sitting beside them to drink it, resting his elbows on the table. It seemed that he could be sociable after all.

"I saw you, I think, at the *Café de Commerce* the other day," he said hesitantly.

Claudine said that they had noticed him too. She wondered whether to go on and say any more but it was all rather awkward. He was such a nice man that you felt you couldn't push and pry. There was something about him that stopped you wanting to do it.

"I once met your mother. A long time ago." They waited, not drinking, not moving. "But I don't suppose she would remember me. She didn't mention me, did she?"

"No," said Claudine truthfully, thinking that if only she had been able to say yes then it might have led on to something else.

He sighed a little; at least, it seemed to them listening so carefully that it was a sigh. It was a small noise accompanied by a small movement of his shoulders and hands. His face had a sad expression.

"It was a nice meal, wasn't it?" said Sophie, wanting to cheer him up. "At the *Café de Commerce*. Did you have the chicken?"

He smiled at her. Yes, he had had the chicken, and it had been very good. The French were such splendid cooks, and he especially liked provincial cooking. He expected that their mother would be a good cook too?

"She's brilliant," said Sophie.

"So is Aunt Nicole," added Claudine with a flash of inspiration. They had forgotten all about Aunt Nicole.

His face seemed to blanch a little. Or was she imagining it again? She seemed to have reached the point where she was imagining people reacting to everything. It was so difficult to know how people were really feeling and to judge how they were responding to what you said. It was so easy to misinterpret.

"You have an aunt?"

Were his long, slender hands trembling? Claudine blinked, trying to focus more clearly, trying to be objective. She told him a bit about Aunt Nicole, how she worked in Paris and was very successful and very fashionable and very gay and very nice.

"Did you ever meet her?" asked Sophie.

"I believe I might have done." He got up now and the moment of intimacy had passed. He wanted them to leave, they knew it, by the way he stood looking out through the open window.

The girls got up, thanking him for the drink. He made them feel very polite and rather grave.

"How long are you staying?" asked Claudine.

The professor turned. "We leave the day after tomorrow," he said in a cool voice.

He accompanied them to the gate, talking formally again, wishing them a good summer in the valley. They were lucky to have such a lovely place in which to spend their summer, he told them, very lucky; they should make the most of it whilst they could be carefree. He undid the latch and the gate swung inwards.

"Goodbye, and thank you again," they called.

As they turned to wave they almost fell over their grandfather coming up the hill.

7

A Visit to Great-aunt Eulalie

PAUL AND CHRISTIAN fished for two hours but caught nothing.

"It is not important," said Christian, laying aside his rod. "To catch, I mean."

"No," agreed Paul, whilst knowing that he would prefer to return triumphant. "Though the girls will crow. Laugh."

Christian smiled. "It must be nice to have sisters. Less lonely."

"I suppose. It has its drawbacks."

"Everything does. No?"

They saw a fish plop in the water. Insects were hovering in thick clouds, and all around came the tic-tic-tic of the cicadas. Paul yawned. He could not understand how Claudine could get so worked up and summon so much energy for her systematic enquiries. The world was so peaceful. He felt sure that there could be nothing sinister to uncover here. And it was unlikely that, no matter what she found out, it would enable Christian to stay on in the valley.

But they must go now, each back to their separate houses, and go separately.

"It seems kind of daft," muttered Paul, "not even to be able to walk along the road together."

Christian nodded. "Paul, what do you think it is, this mystery?"

"I don't know. Probably nothing much. I wish Claudine would

leave well alone. She's always trying to build mountains out of molehills."

"But all is not well, is it? Something *is* wrong."

"You think?" Paul felt more troubled by Christian's apprehension than by his sister's.

"There has been something in my father's life . . . And before we came here he started to talk to me about facing up to things at long last. And then he —" Christian cupped his hands towards one another and brought them close together "— he closed up tight." He gazed downstream without seeing the trees or the rippling water. Then he shrugged. "Tomorrow?"

Paul nodded.

Christian went first; Paul waited for five minutes before he followed. He met no one on the road until he struck off up their own drive. Round the first bend his sisters were waiting under a tree. They both began to talk at once, telling him how they had met and talked and drunk with the professor and actually been inside the house!

"And there was no sign of any bodies or *anything*," said Sophie. "Not even an old bloodstain."

"No, there was nothing like that. And Sophie had a good look, you may be sure of that!"

Paul was impressed by this latest development but became alarmed when he heard that they had met their grandfather outside the house.

"He nearly had a fit," added Sophie, responding to her brother's alarm. "A real fit. Didn't he, Claudine?"

"He didn't look too happy."

"His face went sort of black. It was kind of scarey." Sophie rolled her eyes and put both hands over her heart.

What did Sophie mean exactly, that their grandfather's face had turned black? asked Paul. Black with rage, said Claudine. He had been furious and demanded to know what they were doing in that house. They had told him that Sophie had lost her ball over the hedge and gone to look for it.

"But he muttered all the way down the road," said Sophie. "Using all sorts of swear words and stuff."

"I think he forgot we were there."

"No wonder he was swearing!" said Paul. "Honestly, I don't know how you can be so—" He spluttered to a stop.

"So what?" Claudine eyed him defiantly.

"Insensitive. Unsympathetic."

They continued, without talking, Paul walking a little apart from his sisters and frowning heavily, up the drive.

As they approached the terrace they heard Aunt Nicole's voice.

"Really, Ian, it was a complete waste of time. There was nothing the matter with Aunt Hortense. At least, nothing more than usual."

Aunt Hortense was known for her illnesses, both major and minor. She had had several operations and lived through numerous imaginary ones. Headaches, ear-aches, stomach-aches, pains in the legs, were daily occurrences. Once, when the children had spent a holiday there, they had played at 'Guess what's wrong with Aunt Hortense today'. They had scored five points for a bull's eye, four for a near-miss, and so on. It had been impossible to score nothing.

Aunt Nicole waved to them to come and sit by her.

"So, was it her legs or her stomach?" asked Claudine.

"Both." They laughed, and Aunt Nicole said, "Poor Aunt Hortense! She is a good soul in other ways."

Mrs Grant had been looking pensive. Now she said, "Nicole, don't fly off at me but—"

"What is it now?"

"I promised we'd go to Agen tomorrow."

"To Agen?"

"Aunt Eulalie is expecting us. I promised before we knew we'd have to go to St. Girons."

Aunt Nicole threw up her hands, declaring that she did not mean to budge from the valley. Not a centimetre! She had been looking forward for the last few weeks to lying in the sun doing nothing, listening to the quiet hum of the countryside. She had had her fill of the roar of traffic in Paris and trotting around seeing people. She wanted to see no one now but them. And they had had that hectic drive up and down to the Pyrenees all for nothing. That was enough!

"But I have promised, Nicole. We'll have to go."

"We can phone, put it off for another day."

But their mother insisted that they must go tomorrow. Aunt Eulalie was old and partly deaf and hated to have her routine put out. It seemed so obvious to the children that Aunt Nicole was being kept out of the way. So was it then Aunt Nicole whom the sunflower house concerned?

Whilst Claudine sipped her cool drink she pondered. Christian's half-brother was twenty-two years old. That was a factor she had not taken into account. For surely that meant that the professor had been married for at least twenty-three years? And that would have meant he would have had to have been in love with their mother or aunt when she was sixteen or seventeen years old. She supposed that would have been possible, but not terribly likely. She sighed, scuffed her sandal over the paved stone. It was all rather confusing and the pieces did not seem to fit together too easily. And it was very hot, as if the heat had gathered for the end of the afternoon. She saw a lizard come from under a stone and dart swiftly and gracefully up the wall, to disappear into a crack. How could those little things move so fast in such heat?

Aunt Nicole was speaking to her, asking what she was doing at school. Aunt Nicole seemed to be the only one with any life on this hot afternoon. She looked cool and pretty in pale green. Why had she never married?

When they broke up and Aunt Nicole went inside to help their mother prepare the meal, Claudine wandered down the drive to her grandparents' house. The verandah was empty. She pushed aside the ribboned curtain and entered calling to her grandmother.

"Is that you, Claudine?" Her grandmother came from the bedroom on the ground floor. She put a finger to her lips and led

Claudine back out on to the verandah.

"Your grandfather has just gone to lie down. He has had a funny little turn." She looked worried.

Claudine felt a pang of guilt. "Is he all right?"

"I expect so. He has high blood pressure, you know, he has to watch it. And he is not an easy man when it comes to watching things, you know that too!" And *Grand'mère* smiled.

They sat on the verandah. The shadows were lengthening across the grass in front of the house. Claudine said that it was nice to have Aunt Nicole here.

"Ah yes, she is always gay and full of talk."

"Why did she never marry, *Grand'mère*?"

"Oh, she was engaged once, for two years."

"She was?" Claudine jumped at the news eagerly.

"Yes. To a boy from Montauban."

"Oh."

"And then the engagement was broken."

"Who broke it?"

Aunt Nicole apparently. She had decided that she didn't want to marry the boy after all, but to go to Paris and study design. And so she had gone and become an interior designer. "But she would have been better married. She chose her career instead. Well, I suppose she thought she knew best."

"And perhaps she did."

"A woman is as well married as not. Better, in my opinion."

Claudine did not argue, knowing that her grandmother's opinion would not be changed on that subject, or few others for that matter.

"Mother said to ask if you and *Grand-père* would like to come up for dinner this evening?"

But *Grand'mère* did not wish to, as they had expected. She could not be doing with all that heavy food on her stomach late at night. It wasn't good for you. And anyway, there was *Grand-père* now, needing to rest, not wanting any more excitement for one day. Aunt Nicole should stay with them; she too, since taking to the city, had developed city ways.

Throughout the meal Claudine watched her aunt. Her face was alive and animated, and looked as if it contained no dark mysteries or past pain. But then of course one could never tell by just looking at a face. It was not in Aunt Nicole's nature to go around looking depressed. As the meal progressed, Claudine realised that the next person to be questioned must be Aunt Nicole herself. They had never asked her about the sunflower house, had never thought to somehow, perhaps because they always associated her with Paris. To Claudine she belonged to a narrow street on the Left Bank; here she just seemed like a visitor passing through each summer, like them.

Aunt Nicole was sleeping at the farm. When it was time for her to go, Claudine got to her feet, saying that she would accompany her.

"All right, Claudine, I accept your offer. I am perfectly capable of going home alone but it would be nice to be accompanied."

They set off down the dark drive, Claudine carrying the torch, beaming the light on to the rough ground in front of them, sometimes fanning the hedge on either side so that they might avoid the nastiest of the prickly branches. She must speak to Aunt Nicole now and yet she wished that it was light so that she could watch her face and try to gauge her reactions. But there might not be a better opportunity and, besides, she was much too impatient to wait.

Aunt Nicole slipped her hand through Claudine's arm. She said that the countryside seemed strange and very dark after the lights of the city. It took a bit of getting used to again, that and the quietness, although if you listened you could always hear some kind of noise somewhere.

Claudine took a deep breath. "Aunt Nicole, you know the road up to the church?" Aunt Nicole's fingers stiffened inside her arm: she was sure of it. Or was she waiting for such a reaction?

Yes, she knew that road, Aunt Nicole answered in a casual sort of voice. Too casual, too disinterested, thought Claudine. For as well as sounding casual there had been something wary about her voice.

"There is a house half way up," went on Claudine determinedly. "The garden is full of sunflowers —"

Aunt Nicole cut her short. She said that she believed there was an empty house up there, it had been empty for a long time. She began to speak again of the night, and said to Claudine, "Listen, isn't that a young nightingale?"

"Aunt Nicole, are you sure that you don't know anything about that house?"

"Why should I?"

"Nobody seems to know anything about it. And I can't believe that they don't. There is something wrong with that house, something happened there —"

"It is best not to pry sometimes, Claudine. Do not speak to me of that house, please!" Aunt Nicole's voice was shaking. "Let me enjoy the night instead."

Claudine escorted her aunt the rest of the way to the farmhouse and returned up the hill. She did not use the torch going back, did not need it, for she knew each twist and turn of the drive and after being out for a few minutes her eyes were easily able to detect the lie of the land. She was convinced now that Aunt Nicole was concerned with the mystery.

"You can't be absolutely sure," said Paul, when he came into the girls' room later. "She might just be distressed on *Grand-père's* account. As mother was too."

"I think Aunt Nicole could fall in love with the German professor," said Sophie. "He is a nice man. I could fall in love with him myself. If he was much, much younger of course."

They huddled together on Claudine's bed. It was necessary now to find out some facts, to stop speculating, said Claudine. Her head ached from supposition, like sitting too long over a crossword puzzle. And Christian and his father were to leave the day after tomorrow. Time was running out.

"We *must* find out something more," said Claudine. "I feel it's important."

"Perhaps you're right," said Paul reluctantly. "Perhaps it might be important for Christian and his father, if nothing else."

But what were they to do next? It seemed futile to go on questioning people in the valley; they were all protecting someone, presumably their grandfather.

"You don't mean *Grand-père* was the bad one?" Sophie was shocked.

"Of course not," said Paul abruptly. "He is a very good man, no one could doubt that. You agree on that, don't you, Claudine?"

She thought she did but their father often said that one could never be sure what people were capable of, given the right circumstances.

"*Grand-père* would never do anything bad," said Paul, heatedly now. "He is a good, kind man. He is well respected all over this valley, everyone speaks of him with affection."

When Paul was worked up about something he sounded pompous, thought Claudine, a bit like their accountant grandfather in Edinburgh when he was delivering a lecture. Even in the dim light she could see that her brother's eyes were sparking. She did not tell him that their grandfather was unwell. He would probably have recovered by morning and no one else need worry about him.

"I don't believe the professor is the bad man," said Sophie. "He was very kind to us this afternoon."

"I know," said Claudine suddenly. "Old newspapers! If anything happened it would have been reported there."

"Only if it was a crime," said Paul. "Lots of things — private things — could happen without getting into the newspaper."

Well, it was a chance, wasn't it? It was worth pursuing. They would have to go to Agen to the public library and look through back numbers of the local newspapers. They would ask to go with their mother and aunt to visit Great-Aunt Eulalie. Sophie was not to be included. She would be of little help and they would probably get on faster without her. She should do a little private scouting around at home and keep them informed of what was happening at the sunflower house.

At first she was annoyed but agreed after Claudine pointed out that she would be bored at the library. Also, someone should be on duty in the valley.

"You want to go and visit Aunt Eulalie?" said their mother disbelievingly.

"Well . . ." said Claudine. "As a matter of fact, we want to do some shopping."

"Oh, all right. You can come. But on condition you come to say hello to Aunt Eulalie first."

Great-Aunt Eulalie was about ten years older than their grandmother but seemed to them to be at least double her age. She dressed in a kind of moth colour from head to foot, so that she matched the moth-eaten carpets and velour chairs. Claudine said it was impossible to imagine a more colourless room. Even Aunt Eulalie's skin blended. The sun penetrated only in thin pencils of light where the shutters needed repairing. The house was vast, set behind wrought-iron fences and gates, and the large garden was a wilderness of weeds. She lived there alone, her two other maiden sisters having died some years ago.

Claudine and Paul spent an uncomfortable hour sneezing in the dust of the chairs, shouting answers to Aunt Eulalie's questions, and examining all the pictures on the sitting-room wall which they knew by heart already. They were mostly holy pictures and Aunt Eulalie approved of them giving them such attention.

Even Aunt Nicole could not be gay.

At last their mother released them, saying that they could go to town for a couple of hours, but to be back for lunch. They had brought a picnic to have with Aunt Eulalie.

Outside the gate they breathed the air with relief, and Paul sneezed several times in succession.

"Some picnic it'll be!" said Claudine. "Do you think she *ever* goes out?"

Paul did not care particularly.

The centre of the town was busy with the market. They bought a couple of juicy peaches and ate them before going to the library, and whilst they ate they discussed their approach.

"We can say we're doing a project at school," said Claudine. "A survey of our grandfather's valley. How it was twenty years ago."

Paul said that did not sound very convincing to him. Scathingly, his sister told him to think of a better reason. They were always doing projects at school on such things. He had done one on the Georgian New Town of Edinburgh last year, hadn't he? But here, in France, would they? Oh really! At times he was as cautious as his Edinburgh grandfather. And he could be as cussed as his French one. She considered that he had the worst attributes of both.

"And what about you? You are the family saint, I presume?"

They glowered at one another. Paul threw his peach stone into a waste bin where it landed with an angry rattle.

"Oh, come on," said Claudine, "don't let's fight over it. Let's get on with it."

Paul, without enthusiasm, agreed. Did they need to give a reason at the library? Claudine thought so; they had to ask for the files, could not just walk in and take them. She would feel easier with a prepared excuse.

"Let's go!" She went ahead of him, knowing that if they dithered much more they would never get anywhere.

How far back should they look? She thought maybe twenty-five years.

"If you go back twenty-five years, Aunt Nicole would only have been fifteen. The same age as you! Can you see yourself in love with a German professor?"

"Why not?" she said coolly. "He wouldn't have been a professor, would he, then?"

"I don't suppose so. But somehow I can't see a man like that being in love with you even if he was twenty years younger. Of course Aunt Nicole may have been more mature. Probably was."

He side-stepped to avoid the swift kick he saw travelling towards his ankle.

71

It was quite easy after all. Of course they could have a look at the newspaper files. And how interesting for them to have such a project! Claudine smiled sweetly and said she thought they would start with twenty years ago though it might be necessary for them to dig a little further back, to get the flavour of the period.

They settled down in front of the files, skimming through one old yellowed newspaper after the other, each taking a different file. Their eyes travelled rapidly, taking in headlines and photographs. They resisted the temptation to stop at interesting, irrelevant reports. Nothing anywhere rang a bell. At one point Paul thought he had found something; he caught the name of their valley, but it was only a report about some new farming organisation.

After an hour they were beginning to feel less hopeful. It could easily be a total waste of time and Paul did not believe there was going to be anything in any newspaper about their grandfather, except to announce the birth of his children, and marriage if they went back far enough! But Claudine said they must spend all day here if necessary. The police never gave up on investigations, did they? They went to endless lengths, searched everything, followed every clue. It really was a case of having to sift a haystack to find a needle.

"Patience and perseverance," said Claudine, who was not enormously gifted with either. They were attributes more to be found in her brother.

"We can't spend all day," he reminded her. "Mother said two hours."

"They can have their picnic without us. Let's go back a year."

They began on the new file. Suddenly, Paul saw a familiar face staring up at him. It was a much younger version of his grandfather, one that he had never seen, but it was undeniably him. Black hair, brushed back, small moustache, unsmiling dark eyes. Miserable eyes. The misery was obvious, even in the rather blurred newspaper photograph.

"Claudine," Paul cried out, and then stopped, wishing he could close the paper and let it be buried for ever. For he had just read the caption beneath the photograph.

8

Prospects for Paul

"WHAT IS IT, Paul?"

Paul's face was ashen. He stared and stared at the newspaper, then said, his lips moving slowly, "*Grand-père* was sentenced to three years' imprisonment."

"For what?"

"For shooting —"

"The professor?"

He nodded. Claudine squashed on to the chair beside him and together they read the report. Jean-Paul Vidal had been sentenced to three years' imprisonment for shooting and wounding Professor Otto Brander in the garden at "Mon Repos." That was more or less all the information given.

"I don't believe it," said Paul.

"Paul, it says —"

"We must look back. There'll be earlier reports."

In a daze, they searched back over the previous weeks' issues and put together the facts as best they could. Paul had been working backwards through the paper, having started in December.

It appeared that their grandfather had gone to call on the professor, to discuss the matter of his friendship with his daughter. An argument had ensued and he had become very worked up. It was understandable, his counsel had said, and his strong feelings, both as a father, and a former member of the Resistance, must be respected. Eventually, unable to extract a promise from the professor not to see his daughter again, he had lost his temper. He had just been out hunting, had his gun with him; he raised it to fire over the head of the professor, to frighten him, and then in a state of extreme nervous excitement, he had fired a second shot and hit the professor in the chest. It had not been his intention to kill, or even to harm, him. The regrettable incident had happened because of the temporary derangement of M. Vidal who had been under great emotional strain, claimed his counsel. But whether he had intended to harm the professor or not, the fact remained that he had fired a bullet into a man's chest and it had penetrated the lung. The professor had been rushed to hospital in a critical condition and operated on immediately.

I don't believe it, Paul wanted to say again, but could not, for, in fact, he could believe it only too easily. He accepted that it must be the truth. At least the truth on the whole, though maybe not the whole truth.

"Why didn't he say the gun went off accidentally?" said Claudine. "What an idiot he was to say that he fired initially over the professor's head to frighten him!"

Paul shrugged, did not answer. His head was aching, as if someone had driven a large spike right through the middle of it. He knew well enough why his grandfather would have said what he did. He was not a man to lie, or even avoid the truth, although it might be to save his own skin: it was not in his nature. Discretion would never be the better part of his valour. He had done what he had done and he admitted it; it was not even clear whether he regretted it.

"What an awful thing to do, to shoot at a man, even over his head!"

Paul sighed. It *was* awful. And *Grand-père* might have killed the professor; he was only lucky that he had not.

They replaced the newspapers and left the library. The sun was so bright in the street that it startled them; they felt as if they had been sitting in thick gloom for several hours. Claudine took out her sun-glasses and covered her eyes, glad to have something to hide behind.

Still dazed, and without saying a word to one another, they walked back to Aunt Eulalie's house.

They were in the middle of their picnic which had been spread upon Aunt Eulalie's vast velour-covered dining-room table. Paté, chicken and cheese had been laid on greenish-looking silver platters.

"You're late," said their mother.

"Sorry," mumbled Claudine and slipped into a chair. She stared at the food. "I'm not hungry."

Aunt Eulalie shook her head and said that she should not have been out in the hot sun without a hat. In her opinion it was a mistake to go into the sun at all, but especially when it was at its height at midday.

"Aren't you going to eat anything?" Mrs Grant looked from one to the other.

They shook their heads.

"Oh, well!"

They noticed that neither their mother nor their aunt were eating all that much themselves. Who would want to, thought Claudine, after it had been on that mouldy silver? Except for Aunt Eulalie who was used to it. What was left over would last her for a week.

Mercifully, their mother decided they should leave soon after lunch. She wanted to visit a cousin a mile out of town.

"Another visit," groaned Claudine.

"Annie has several children, they must all be teenagers now." Mrs Grant appeared to think that would make up for Aunt Eulalie.

Aunt Nicole exploded when they got into the car.

"Really, Françoise, I have had enough! I want to go home. Ever since I got down here I have not had one minute's peace. It might amuse you to spend your entire time paying calls on our relations but it does not me!"

"Oh, come on, Nicole, you like Annie."

"But not today."

But her sister had made up her mind, and once that happened little would shift it, as her children knew. She drove, with Aunt Nicole protesting beside her, to the house of Annie and her many teenage children. Her own two sat in the back of the car saying nothing.

"You always have to have your own way, Françoise."

By the time they reached Annie's house no one was talking.

The house was modern, gleaming white with bright turquoise shutters and black curlicued wrought-iron balconies. Beside it glittered a kidney-shaped swimming pool the same colour as the shutters. Annie's husband was a wealthy industrialist. Aunt Eulalie, who had never made any marriage herself, had not been able to understand why Françoise and Nicole could not have made such good marriages. A teacher of drawing from Scotland indeed!

The shutters were closed, the garden empty, the pool unruffled. Mrs Grant got briskly out of the car and marched up the path to the front door. She pulled the wrought-iron bell-handle. The three in the car watched. After a moment she pulled again, more firmly, aggressively almost, and waited, with her back to them.

"It would appear that Annie is not at home," said Aunt Nicole, who was smiling.

Their mother came slowly back to the car glancing up and down the street in case Annie and her brood might loom over the horizon at any moment. But they did not.

"Perhaps now we may go home?" said Aunt Nicole.

Mrs Grant drove a little faster than usual, clipping the corners of the narrow roads a little too finely. Low hanging branches slapped their windscreen. Paul and Claudine gazed out at passing farmhouses, little churches, fields of corn, without seeing them.

Half-way home, Paul was sick.

"You haven't been car-sick for a long time," said his mother, after she had cleaned up the mess and he had sat by the road for a few minutes to recover. "Aunt Eulalie must have been right. Too much sun!"

She drove more slowly the rest of the way.

Aunt Nicole accompanied them up to the house and she and her sister went inside. Claudine and Paul slipped round the back to look for Sophie.

They found her sitting on an old tree stump behind the *pigeonnier*. She began to chatter as soon as she saw them, not noticing their mood. She had been to visit Professor Brander again! What did they think of that then? They seemed to think nothing; they stared at her.

"He was terribly nice to me, gave me some more cold lemon and a biscuit."

"That's good," said Claudine.

"Are you feeling sick or something?"

A bit, answered Claudine, collapsing on to the ground where she sat holding her knees up to her chin. Paul was watching a black and white butterfly flitting up and over the grass, stopping to touch the cornflowers. It must be nice to be a butterfly, to be so light and able to flit here and there, without thinking, without having to know things.

"We got talking quite a bit." Sophie waited for their reaction but, again, none came. Paul had now joined Claudine on the ground and was chewing a piece of grass. Below they could see the roof of their grandparents' farmhouse.

"He asked all about Aunt Nicole," said Sophie, bringing out her trump card and laying it in front of them.

At this they did look up. Was that right? asked Claudine. Sophie had not imagined it or brought up the subject first herself? Sophie shook her head emphatically, declaring that he had asked what had happened to her aunt. She added, "He asked me if she was married."

"I dare say he just wanted to be brought up to date with the news," said Claudine.

"I think he was in love with Aunt Nicole," said Sophie. "He looked kind of in love when he talked about her."

"I expect he thought it would be safe to talk to you," said Paul. "Little did he know!"

"Probably thought I'd be too young to know what he was getting at." Sophie grinned.

Paul got up saying he'd be seeing them. He went down through the wood at the side of the drive. He needed some time on his own to try to come to terms with what they had found out in the library at Agen. He still felt staggered by it. He had always looked up to his grandfather, had thought of him as someone special; he had known that he could get excited and lose his temper but that had never mattered much. But shooting at someone did.

He kicked at a tuft of grass. Why had Claudine insisted on poking and prying! Why not let sleeping dogs lie? At times it seemed to him that was the more sensible course. What good would it do them having this piece of information? All it had done so far was make them feel miserable, and he knew that he would never be able to look at his grandfather again in quite the same way as before.

"Paul!" A voice calling startled him. It was his grandfather's voice.

He came to the edge of the wood and saw that the old man was standing on the verandah of the farmhouse.

"Ah, there you are! I thought I saw you moving through the trees." He beckoned to him. "Come here, I want to talk to you."

Paul's heart lurched. Could he have found out that they had found out? *Grand-père* seemed to have an uncanny knack of finding things out.

He shinned over the fence, crossed the drive and jumped down into the garden. He looked across at his grandfather feeling as if he had a golf ball lodged in his throat. No matter what he had done, he was still a fine old man and he was glad that he was his grandfather! Paul went to him.

"How are you, *Grand-père*?"

"All right, all right. Just had a little bit of a funny turn, that was

79

all. All this fussing . . . Women! Come on, Paul, sit down. I have things to say to you."

They took seats side by side on the verandah. For a few minutes they sat in silence looking out across the farm. Paul felt that his grandfather really was looking at the farm, taking in each detail.

"My family have farmed in this valley for a long time. My father and his father . . ." He paused. Paul nodded but did not speak.

"I have no sons. My daughters are no farmers."

Paul smiled.

"I have you, Grandson."

"Yes, *Grand-père*. And I—"

"You want to be a farmer?"

"Yes, I do."

"You think that you could come here and live like a Frenchman? You have been brought up to be a Scotsman."

"There is not too much difference, *Grand-père*. It would not change me either way. I love this valley, I would like to be a farmer here too."

The old man nodded. "Very well. I have been watching you every summer, I feel the land is in your blood too. It has come out in you, not in your mother who went away, nor in your aunt who has forsaken us for Paris. The farm will pass to you, Paul. I will keep it warm for you, until you are ready."

"Thank you, *Grand-père*."

And that was all. No song and dance. The exchange had been cool, calm, unemotional. It was strange, since his grandfather could be so emotional.

His grandmother emerged from the ribboned curtain, carrying a tray with a bottle and glasses. "You will take a glass of wine with your grandfather, Paul?"

"Please."

His grandmother poured two glasses of red wine and they drank, raising their glasses to one another. They knew what it was they were drinking to, but not a word was said. *Grand-mère*, standing behind them in her navy-blue dress, knew also and was glad.

No more was said, no plans were laid. It would all happen in its own good time.

After a second glass of wine, Paul walked unsteadily up the drive. On the way he passed Aunt Nicole coming down. She said that she was going to lie in the grass and go to sleep. The air was very thick and heavy, almost as if a storm threatened.

His mother had gone to take a nap also, in her bedroom, and his father was asleep in a deck-chair with a hat over his face and a towel over his feet. Paul broke off a piece of bread and ate it dry, feeling better almost as soon as the food touched his stomach. Then he took a drink of Vichy water from the fridge.

Vichy! What associations that conjured up for him now!

His sisters were still beside the *pigeonnier*. Claudine had told Sophie what they had discovered in Agen. Her eyes were enormous.

"Claudine says that *Grand-père* was almost a murderer?"

"Of course he was not!" Paul spoke hotly. "Even if he had killed the professor it would only be manslaughter." Only!

"That's not very nice though, is it?"

Paul shrugged. He had to admit that it was not. His head still ached, had done since morning. Too much had happened to him in one day and he felt he could not keep pace with it all.

"Let's go to the river," he said. They collected their things and as soon as they arrived he plunged straight into the cold running water face downward, keeping it there until he gasped for air and had to roll round on to his back. He wished that the river could cleanse all knowledge from him, carry it away and leave him empty to watch the green branches against the blue sky. He wanted nothing more. He did not want to know about his grandfather. But he did know and could not pretend that he did not.

Claudine, miserable, waded towards him, the current pulling against her thighs. "I'm sorry, Paul. You were right. I am far too nosey."

It was not her fault, said Paul; it was not she who had shot anyone. It was wrong to kill, quite wrong, and they could not

81

excuse their grandfather. And yet he loved the old man, more than ever. Yes, he realised with surprise, he did, more than ever.

Christian came soon, greeting them brightly, seeming to be more talkative than he had ever been before. He had hoped to find them here. At each meeting they found that he loosened up a little more and they knew that if they spent the whole summer together they would end up as close friends. But they were not to have the chance to stay together all summer for Christian was due to leave the following day.

He was smiling. "There is a reprieve."

Paul started, thinking Christian meant their grandfather. But Christian was referring to his departure from the valley. His father had decided to wait a few more days, to do one or two other jobs in the house.

"I bet that's because I told him Aunt Nicole was here," said Sophie.

"Christian, it seems we were wrong about your father and our mother." said Claudine. "We believe that your father was in love with our Aunt Nicole at one time. Can you understand how that can be, since your half-brother is twenty-two and Aunt Nicole is only forty?"

It happened that Christian's half-brother was the son of his mother by a previous marriage, not his father, as they had thought. "My mother and father married seventeen years ago, I think."

"Ah, that explains it! Your father met Aunt Nicole before that then."

"You know that?"

They told him what they knew, and after the telling they were silent for a few minutes. The river rushed by, the birds twittered, and the cicadas chirped, as usual.

"Perhaps you'll hate us now," said Sophie, breaking the silence. "Since our grandfather shot your father."

Christian blinked. "Why should I hate you? It has nothing to do with me or us. What my father and your grandfather did before us."

That was true, agreed Paul, in a way; yet, on the other hand, they were involved with that. For wasn't that the reason that they were not supposed to meet one another? It was still something that would upset their grandfather today. As well it might, thought Paul.

"I do not resent your grandfather either," said Christian. "We do not understand enough about it."

"That's true," said Claudine slowly. "We don't know enough."

They would confront their parents with it that evening. They must. And Christian said that he would speak to his father.

Aunt Nicole did not come up to their house that evening; she stayed below at the farm with her mother and father. Mrs Grant looked tired. She said that it had been a somewhat tiring day, had it not? She always found a visit to Aunt Eulalie's moth-eaten house quite enervating. She thought if she stayed very long in it she would soon look moth-eaten too.

"Sit down, Mother," said Claudine. "You take a rest and I'll cook the dinner."

"I'll help," said Paul.

What was the matter with them? They must have been too long in the sun! Their mother laughed and relaxed a little, sitting down under the umbrella on the terrace with an aperitif.

They cooked a good meal and set it out nicely on the table. Claudine made a menu as they did in restaurants and decorated it round the edges with drawings of peaches, plums, tomatoes and peppers. By the time they had finished eating their mother seemed to have completely recovered from her trip to Agen. Their father too, after food and a good bottle of wine, was in a mellow mood and smoking a cigar, which he did from time to time.

"We want to ask you something," said Claudine. "And we hope that you will answer us honestly."

"Sounds serious," said their father lazily, not taking her statement too seriously.

Paul hesitated. "It is about *Grand-père* and the German professor."

Mrs Grant was looking at her husband.

"You will have to tell them, Françoise," he said. "It's better that they know now, they're old enough. And it seems to me that they must know a certain amount already."

"What *do* you know?" she asked.

They told her. She sighed and leaned back in her chair. Obviously there was nothing else to be done now but to tell them the whole story.

Otto Brander, Christian's father, had come to the valley twenty-one years ago. He had bought the house below the church and come to spend the summer there. He was writing a book. And he was thirty years old, attractive and unmarried.

Nicole was then twenty years old. She was a beautiful girl, with long chestnut hair and a gay laugh. She met the professor in the churchyard up on the hill. They fell in love. It was a very basic, simple story, said their mother, but it could not remain simple because of the implications. Otto was German and Nicole French, and her father could not approve of that liaison.

It was not long before he found out. Secrets were difficult in a valley such as this. He was furious with his daughter and demanded that she did not see the German again. He told her that she knew how much he hated the Boche and how much it would hurt him if she were ever to marry one. She protested in vain, telling him that Otto was no criminal, no Nazi, but a good fine man. Her father would not listen, did not want to listen, and even her mother advised her that it would be better to break off the relationship before it caused too much trouble. But Nicole decided that she would not break off her friendship with Otto. She felt that her father was unreasonable and should try to be less prejudiced. They argued bitterly and fell out.

And then came the day of the shooting. It was September, and the hunting season. Coming back late one afternoon with his gun, Nicole's father stopped by the German's house. He intended to talk to him, to ask him to go away and leave his daughter alone.

"My father said that he didn't intend to harm Otto when he went there." Mrs Grant's voice wavered slightly now. "But he lost his temper – you know how excitable he is – well, you know the rest." She got up and walked over to the window. Her face was brooding, her eyes had a faraway look, as if she was back in that time of twenty-one years ago. "I think that he *did* want to kill him – at that moment anyway."

"No!" cried Paul, horrified to hear put into words what he himself feared.

No one answered him.

It must have been a terrible time, thought Claudine, for all of them. Their mother, Aunt Nicole, and of course *Grand'mère*. To have her husband charged and sentenced and committed to prison!

He had served only two years, then been released for good behaviour. But he had come out of prison very bitter, his hatred of Germans reinforced, for hadn't it been on account of one that he had had to go to prison? He was not the most rational of men.

Their mother turned. "On that whole matter nothing would ever change him. Nothing! And we can do nothing about it. We must accept him as he is."

Paul nodded. His throat was too dry to speak.

And Aunt Nicole? asked Claudine. What had she done?

She had given up Otto, for that had seemed to her the only thing to be done. Her friendship with him had caused enough pain already, too much, and she blamed herself greatly that she had not broken off with Otto when her father had first asked her. She felt that she had been stubborn to pursue it against all the odds.

"But that's ridiculous," cried Claudine. "She loved him. And he loved her."

Their mother said that that did not always justify going ahead, not if other people were to be hurt too badly. Claudine could not see it, for they had spoiled their own happiness. Their mother shrugged. Otto Brander had gone back to Germany and married and had a son. But Aunt Nicole never married, countered Claudine.

"She had her career. That was what she wanted."

"How do you know?"

"No more questions now, children," said their father. "I think your mother's had enough."

"You must promise not to speak of it to your Aunt Nicole."

They promised.

"You too, Sophie!"

Sophie raised two fingers in the Brownie salute. "I promise."

"And you must promise not to tell her that Otto Brander is back in the valley!"

They gave their promises again, Claudine with reluctance.

"We are doing everything we can to keep her away from there. We are hoping that the Branders will leave very soon."

They did not tell her that Professor Brander had only just decided to stay on for a few more days. There were things it was better for her not to know. They went to bed, gathering in the girls' room by the open window. The air was so close and oppressive that they needed to get whatever breath of wind was stirring.

They leant their elbows on the sill and gazed out over the valley. They could see the light of their grandparents' farmhouse below, and a little bit further over on the hill, the light of the sunflower house. Would Aunt Nicole not see that too? Probably not, down in the valley.

"Must we keep our promise?" asked Sophie.

"There are indirect ways of doing things," said Claudine.

"And what does that mean?" asked Paul.

"It means that I am thinking," said Claudine, her eyes fixed steadily on the small light that marked the place of the professor's house.

9

Aunt Nicole is Taken on a Picnic

THEY WERE WAKENED during the night by enormous claps of thunder overhead and shafts of white light shooting through the holes in the shutters. The noise was enormous. Claudine got up and opened the shutters so that she could watch the storm rage over the valley. She loved electric storms and it was only ever here in summer that they had them quite so vivid and exciting. Sophie, liking them less, huddled under the bedclothes, half enthralled, half terrified. She was certain that the roof was going to come in on top of them.

Claudine gazed out at the valley, dark one moment, brightly-lit the next, almost as it was at noonday.

There was forked lightning as well as sheet; it snaked across the hillside like a darting serpent. The valley looked weird, when normally it was so open and placid and smiling. She always thought of the valley as if it was smiling. And down there, perhaps watching the storm also, were her grandfather, Aunt Nicole, and Professor Brander.

She needed a plan. She could not *tell* Aunt Nicole about the professor, but a meeting could be arranged. That would not be breaking the promise. Not literally, said a voice in her head, but the end result would be the same. She pushed the voice aside, thinking of Christian and his father. They had a quality of loneliness about them which made her want to help them.

"Shut the shutters, please, Claudine," pleaded Sophie.

"The lightning can't touch you. It's over on the other side of the valley anyway."

"You don't know," wailed Sophie, burrowing deeper.

Claudine knew what she would do. She would take Aunt Nicole on a picnic!

The door opened and in came their father, barefooted and in pyjamas. "Quite a storm. Are you two all right?"

"I'm not," said Sophie, poking her head out of the bedcovers. "Can I come in with you?"

"Chancer! Come on then." He bent down and Sophie climbed on his back and he took her away.

So Claudine was left alone. That suited her since she needed peace to perfect her plan and also in which to enjoy the storm properly.

It lasted for another hour or so and was followed by steady rain that rattled on the roof tiles, hissed on the window sill and soaked the floor in front of the window. Claudine heard her father moving about overhead putting buckets to catch the drips. To the sound of the rain she drifted back into sleep.

In the morning she sent Sophie up the hill with a message for Christian. As far as the professor was concerned, Sophie was an accepted caller. Claudine herself made up a picnic and set off with Paul to call on Aunt Nicole. He came a little reluctantly, muttering his usual protests.

"I tell you, Claudine, we should leave well alone."

"You sound middle-aged!"

"Perhaps just sensible."

"Anyway," said Claudine defiantly, needing to speak with certainty since she was not totally sure that she was on the right course, "they should at least be given the chance to meet. To be able to talk over the past."

"Is that a good idea?" Paul kicked a stone down the drive in front of them.

"It might lay ghosts."

"If they've any to lay."

"Christian seems to think his father has. And thinking back on Aunt Nicole all these years – I think she has too. There's always been a feeling of. . . . Well, something not quite sorted out about her. Do you know what I mean?"

"You could say that about nearly everyone."

Everyone but their grandmother, thought Paul, as he pursued the stone. A game of football would be a nice idea. At least it was straightforward and there were rules. His grandmother alone of all the people he knew seemed very sure, as if in the middle of her she knew who she was. She was seldom agitated, fussed or restless. Perhaps his father was pretty sure too. You never felt doubtful about him. But then he might feel doubtful about himself at times. Paul waited for Claudine to catch up.

"There was a great philosopher called Jung," she said.

"I *have* heard of him," said Paul, who had, just.

"He said that the older he got the only thing he was sure of was that he wasn't sure of anything."

"Not much help, is it?"

"I don't know. Perhaps it just means you shouldn't be too bothered when you don't feel absolutely sure about something. Accept it."

They had reached the farm gate. One of the dogs came barking to meet them, but stopped as soon as he recognised them. Paul patted his head.

Aunt Nicole was lying under a chestnut tree reading a thriller.

"Bliss," she said, waving the book in greeting. "Nothing to do."

"We've come to take you for a picnic," said Claudine.

"A picnic? Oh dear –"

"We won't go far," Claudine reassured her. "And we have lots of cold drinks with us."

Aunt Nicole gave in, throwing up her hands in mock horror. Everyone wanted to organise her. Even today her father had wanted her to drive all the way up to Perigord on some errand or other, something quite unimportant. She had simply refused. But a picnic along the valley . . . Oh well, that might be rather nice. And besides, she had not had much time to talk to them yet.

Sophie came running, panting. "That child!" Aunt Nicole shook her head. "Such energy."

Sophie was grinning. "Mission accomplished." She saluted.

"And what is that supposed to mean?"

"Just part of Sophie's nonsense," said Claudine. "You know she lives in a kind of cloud-cuckoo land."

Sophie stuck out her tongue at her sister, making her aunt laugh.

They set off carrying the hamper and a blanket. Aunt Nicole was not allowed to carry anything except her suntan oil.

They turned right when they left the farm and set off along the road in the direction that led to the lake, and then a little way along they took the first turning on the left up the other side of the hill. At a shady dell just before the brow they stopped; here they could see right down the valley. The view was similar to the one from their own house except of course that it was on the other side. They could see their own house from here, white walls and red pantiles shining in the sun, and there was their father moving about.

Claudine unpacked the hamper. They ate and drank, although Claudine found it difficult to swallow too much. She had a nervous flutter in her tummy. Aunt Nicole declared that it was a delicious picnic and she was glad she had come.

At midday the church bell began to toll. They stopped talking to listen.

"Dear old Madame Grenier never misses," said Aunt Nicole. "How nice to be here! I love this place."

"Not to live in all the year round?" asked Paul.

No, perhaps not, she conceded. Claudine said that Paul was thinking of coming to live here all year round, when he was older.

"I'm sure the life would suit you, Paul. It would be nice to know that someone in the family is going to carry on. And we'll all be able to come and spend summers with you."

After covering her arms and legs with suntan oil she went out into the full glare of the sun to lie down. She said that she wanted to take a nice tan back to Paris with her.

About ten minutes later Claudine asked if she would fancy a walk. She murmured that she wouldn't fancy it at all, she was quite happy to lie where she was, thank you very much. "You are mad, you English. Wanting to go running about in the heat of the day."

Scottish, they all three automatically protested, even Sophie who was lying on her tummy gazing through the stalks of grass half-asleep. Paul wondered why they should insist so much on that when, on the other hand, he often declared that to be French or Scottish or anything else made no difference.

"I wasn't suggesting rushing around," said Claudine. "I only had a gentle stroll in mind."

Her aunt said that she knew what their idea of a gentle stroll was. She had been caught by that before! Claudine said that she wanted to show her something, something interesting.

"*Please*, Aunt Nicole."

Aunt Nicole sat up. She might have known that she wouldn't have been allowed to come on a lazy picnic. They were always so restless, the three of them, going hither and thither. Oh, well!

Grumbling good-naturedly she trailed off with Claudine, leaving the others with the picnic basket. As soon as they were out of sight Paul quickly got up and hastened back down the hill towards his grandfather's house where he was to keep guard and make sure that neither of his grandparents left the premises. It was extremely unlikely that they would at this time of day but, as Claudine said, in order to make sure that a plan was foolproof they must take into account that unexpected things could happen. He squatted in the long grass at the edge of the road where he could keep an eye on the verandah. It was empty: his grandparents would be in the kitchen eating lunch.

Sophie stayed with the picnic rug and hamper, as instructed. It was not much to her liking, just to be left sitting without anything

91

else to do. It was *not* fair: Claudine always got the best bits of the action.

Claudine led her aunt along the top road that led to the church. This was the back way, a narrow road little used except by the local farmer on this side of the valley and by the Greniers.

"Where are you taking me? What is it you've got to show me? You look as if you're full of secrets."

"Wait and see!"

The church was in view ahead of them all the time: small and sturdy with its Romanesque tower standing against the sky. And beside it stood the old presbytery.

They moved slowly, the sun being too high and hot for speed. Surreptitiously, Claudine eyed her watch. Christian should be approaching too now from the other road, with his father. Three minutes to go.

Close to the church the trees were high and overhung the road, giving shade. After the fierce beat of the sun it was agreeable to enter the dim patch of roadway. They came to the wrought-iron railing that surrounded the back of the church and graveyard. Here, their ancestors were buried. Claudine hated the graveyard because of the gaudy artificial flowers on the tombs. It was something that she could not understand. The church was so pretty and unfussy that she could not see why people had to fill the graveyard with such monstrous things. They were bright red, purple and orange, and they glistened waxily. It was the same in all the small churchyards round about.

They were walking along the side of the graveyard with the church on their left. Claudine had that funny feeling back in the pit of her stomach, as if it might turn right over. She might be doing something terrible but it was too late now to go back, to say to Aunt Nicole that she had made a mistake, she had nothing to show her. The shutters of the presbytery were tightly closed; the Parisians were not in residence.

On her left she glimpsed two heads at the far side of the churchyard. Aunt Nicole had not seen them for she was gazing ahead at the presbytery, talking about it, recalling the last *curé* who had been there, saying what a shame it was that the valley could no longer have its own priest.

"This way," said Claudine in a hoarse voice. She cleared her throat, observing how dusty the road was. There had been little rain in weeks, apart from last night's downpour.

Christian and his father must have moved around the back of the church for she could no longer see them.

"Is it something in here, Claudine? In the graveyard?"

Claudine nodded.

At that moment Christian appeared around the side of the church, alone. He came past Claudine and her aunt, nodding, saying, "*Bonjour.*" He continued on down the road as if Claudine was only an acquaintance to be nodded at.

"Who was that boy? I don't think I know him?"

"Go round the back of the church, Aunt Nicole." Claudine spoke rapidly. "I hope it will be all right. Forgive me if it's not." And then she ran off at full tilt down the hill after Christian.

When she reached the gate of the sunflower house she found him standing there waiting for her. They did not speak to one another but gazed back up the hill.

Nothing stirred on the road. A giant bird, some kind of bird of prey, passed overhead, casting a shadow on the sunlit road. From down below in the valley they heard a car pass on the road. Claudine swallowed. Her throat felt painful, as if swollen inside.

They stood there for more than ten minutes. And then they turned to one another.

"They must have met by now," said Christian haltingly. "And Father has not returned."

"Shall we go?"

They went on down the road to join the one that ran along the bottom of the valley. Sophie would have packed up the hamper and rug and proceeded by now to their private stretch of river. They found Paul still squatting on guard. He said that he would remain for another half hour, then he too would join them.

Sophie was polishing off the last of the lunch when they arrived. For once Claudine did not object; her appetite had not recovered anyway. They sat on the bank dabbling their feet in the water, talking very little. Their minds were up in the church on the hill, in the graveyard with its gaudy floral tributes. Claudine wished that she was a butterfly that could flit up the hill into the graveyard and rest on a flower and watch what was happening. She burned with curiosity.

Paul came, saying that no one was moving in their grandfather's house. He was certain that both of the old folk must be fast asleep. The valley seemed asleep, he said, there wasn't a tractor or workman to be seen or heard.

Suddenly, the sky grew dark overhead. It was almost as though someone had flicked a switch and extinguished the sun. A clap of thunder cracked above them, followed by a quick zig-zag of lightning.

"I thought we'd have another storm," said Paul. "We had better get away from the water. And the trees."

Another clap of thunder, another fork of lightning, then more thunder and more lightning again. The storm seemed to be raging right over the valley.

Large spots of rain came splashing through the trees. They scurried away from the river out on to the open road seeking shelter. One of their grandfather's barns would be the ideal place, said Paul, leading the way. They settled themselves down in a bed of hay. From there it was safe and yet exciting to witness the storm.

The rain, when it came, was thick and solid, enclosing them, reducing the outside world to a wavering green blur. Aunt Nicole and Christian's father would have had to take shelter too. The church was kept locked, was opened up only at noonday and for weddings and funerals. And there was no one at the presbytery to offer a refuge, so they could not go there. So unless they went to the Greniers', which was not very probable, they would have had to go to the sunflower house.

Sophie Spills the Beans

THE FOLLOWING DAY, Aunt Nicole went off in her Renault to visit an old school friend at Montauban, or so *Grand'mère* told Claudine. She said that it was very nice to keep up with one's old friends, Nicole had always done it, and so had their mother.

"She will have a good time with Lorraine." *Grand'mère* went on to muse about Lorraine, what a pretty girl she had been, how well she had married and what lovely children she had had. "It's a pity about Nicole . . ." She shrugged.

"Perhaps she will still get married."

But *Grand'mère* did not appear to think so, not at her time of life, when she was used to so much freedom, having her own way. Look at the way she went gadding around Europe, to this capital and that, ski-ing in the wintertime in the Alps!

Christian reported that his father had set off in his little red Volkswagen that morning, informing him that he had much business to do in town and might not be back until late.

"I assured him that I would be quite all right," said Christian with a smile.

Sophie gave a skip. "They must have gone to meet one another."

"It rather looks it," said Claudine. "You see, Paul, it *was* the right thing to do. They obviously wanted to see one another."

"We must wait and see."

Paul went off to help his grandfather on the farm. The old man still felt a bit shaky on his legs, he said; of course he was not young any more and what could you expect? All that day, as they moved around the farm, his grandfather told Paul what would happen when he came. "You will do this when you come here." The theme of Paul's coming seemed to be running through the old man's mind. At one point it seemed to Paul that his grandfather expected him to come fairly soon, that he did not fully realise that it would be four years at least before he could.

"The men will stay," said his grandfather. "They are good workers. They will stick by you. You are a Vidal."

Paul ate lunch with his grandparents also. It seemed as if a new order had been established, as if his grandmother too thought he had become a part of the household. In one way he wished it were possible that he could come and live in the Lot now; on the other hand, when he thought back to Edinburgh, his school, friends, playing rugby, he still wanted to do all of those things, and was not ready yet to leave them.

"I always knew you were one of us," said his grandmother, as she set a large plate of veal stew in front of him at midday. "I knew it from the very beginning. I wasn't deceived that you looked like your father, oh no."

Paul tackled the stew, knowing that he would have to leave a clean plate behind. His grandmother pressed large hunks of fresh bread upon him. Eat up, she commanded him; one had to be strong to work on a farm. It was a long day and there was never any let up, year in, year out. It was all right for those without beasts, but when you had cows to milk then they could never be left. His grandparents had not had a holiday together as far back as they could remember.

I will take holidays, thought Paul, as he wiped his plate obediently with the bread. He would get the farmhands to take over at a time of year when the work was not too hard and he would return to Scotland, to visit his family and friends. He did not intend to turn his back completely on his homeland.

Grand-père sat back in his old winged armchair, and clasped his hands in front of his stomach. He looked more contented today, more at peace. Then Paul thought of Aunt Nicole and Christian's father and laid down his fork. He felt troubled, uneasy in the centre of himself. It was like waiting for another storm to break. Could history repeat itself, as they said? *Grand-père* still had a gun; was still emotional, and still hated Germans. Nothing had changed except that they were all twenty-one years older.

The girls spent their day at the lake with Christian. They felt like having a decent swim for a change, being able to stretch their arms wide and take a few strokes without stumbling on the bottom, and to be able to dive from the edge. And all the time, whether they were swimming or lying in the sun or eating, the same thought ran as an undercurrent in all of their minds: Aunt Nicole and Christian's father were together.

Aunt Nicole came to dinner that evening. She was wearing a white silk dress which looked magnificent against her brown skin, and her face was radiant. It was like a blinding light, the way she smiled, the way she talked so gaily.

"And how was Lorraine?" asked her sister.

Lorraine? Oh, she was fine, just fine. Aunt Nicole passed over Lorraine to talk about the day, how beautiful it was, how much she loved this whole area. Claudine and Paul exchanged looks.

The next day Aunt Nicole set off in her little green Renault to visit an old school friend in Valence d'Agen on the Garonne. Christian reported that his father had gone off in his little red Volkswagen to conduct yet more business.

The Grants spent the morning with Christian but at lunch-time their parents said that they thought they would take a run down to Lamagistère. Claudine looked at Paul. It was a small village on the Garonne, not very far from Valence. Could it be that their parents had any suspicion or was it just coincidence? Coincidence, decided Claudine, for her mother and father had shown no signs whatsoever that they suspected Nicole had seen the professor, and they

97

often went to Lamagistère in the course of a summer.

Christian would have to spend the afternoon alone but they could not do anything about it. They could not ask to bring him thought they wished that they could. But they felt they would have to go themselves in case of complications.

As soon as they reached Lamagistère they went into the river. The drive down had been hot and their thighs had stuck to the car's leather seats. Claudine struck out for the middle feeling the current pulling her strongly downstream. The current was always strong but quite safe. She flipped over on her back and as she did so caught sight of a flash of white further down the bank. It was Aunt Nicole's white dress.

Her father came up behind her throwing the ball overarm. "Catch!"

She went for it. He trod water, and she saw the moment that he saw Aunt Nicole. His face altered. He had a face that showed everything.

"River smells a bit today," he said. "Think we might give it a miss perhaps."

It often smelt strongly and he had often declared that it was nothing but a good healthy river smell. Claudine followed him back to the beach whispering urgently to Paul and Sophie to follow and say nothing. "Disaster threatens. A hundred feet down river."

Sophie's eyes widened and her mouth opened.

"Shut up now, Sophie!"

"I thought we might go up to Puymirol, Françoise," Mr Grant was saying to his wife.

She objected, saying that she was comfortable here, did not feel like moving.

"The river's smelling rather much." His face was dark pink and he was not looking at his wife. "I don't feel like staying here."

She gazed up at him from her deck-chair, mildly surprised. He was not a man of sudden notions. "Oh, sit down, Ian, do! You are much too restless."

He seized on that. Yes, it was true, he admitted, he could not sit still for long, and he wanted to go and photograph the hilltop town of Puymirol. It was such a lovely little town, with the archway running all round the central *place* and the geraniums . . . Meanwhile, he kept glancing jerkily to his left.

"Yes, let's go to Puymirol," said Claudine, gathering up her belongings. They must leave before their father gave Aunt Nicole away completely. Really, he was bad at hiding things! "I'd like to."

But she had been often to Puymirol, said her mother, and it was a hot day for sightseeing. They all wished to go, it seemed, so, protesting, she packed up her bag and returned to the stuffy car.

"You are all mad," she declared, as she settled herself on the hot seat. "You should all remain in Scotland and run up and down hills all day long. This country is too civilised for you."

As they moved up the slope back to the road Claudine saw something white coming round the bend of the beach. Aunt Nicole was looking up into the professor's face and did not see them, and their mother, who was staring grimly ahead, did not see the two people on the sand.

Their father did not say anything to them about having seen Aunt Nicole and they did not say anything to him. He shot off almost a whole reel of film at Puymirol with the air of a man whose mind was not at all on what he was doing.

"All these secrets are becoming difficult to keep," sighed Sophie. "At times I feel I am bursting."

She had better not burst, Claudine warned her. Think of all the trouble there would be if she was to!

Sophie said haughtily that Claudine did not need to worry: of course she would not give anything away.

That evening Claudine managed to get her father alone. They went walking in the damson wood together behind the house and she told him she had seen her aunt at Lamagistère.

"You did? Your mother didn't though, and I don't want her to know. I'm worried, Claudine, about what might happen. I don't know what Nicole's up to—" He frowned.

Claudine picked a damson that was growing wild, put it into her mouth and sucked, enjoying the bitter flesh. She spat out the stone.

"Perhaps they've fallen in love again, Dad. They might never have fallen out."

Her father said that people didn't often stay in love for twenty years, not when they didn't see one another in between. That was asking a bit much of anyone. But he did agree that perhaps, meeting again. . . . It would have been much better, however, if they had not.

Claudine felt guilty but kept quiet. If he knew that she had engineered the meeting!

"What are you going to do?" she asked.

Nothing, he thought. He did not know what to do; he certainly was not going to tell either their mother or grandfather. Nicole and the German professor were old enough and wise enough, he hoped, to manage their own affairs and he must leave them to it.

Claudine nodded. "It is really up to them, isn't it, Dad?"

Whatever might happen would be their choice, their responsibility. No, perhaps that was not quite true, but she wanted it to be true.

Again, that evening, Aunt Nicole was smiling and gay. She had brought with her two bottles of champagne. Just because she felt like it, she told her sister, no special reason. Her sister was the only one who believed her.

Claudine slept badly that night. Once or twice she wakened and got up and crept to the window, easing back the shutter to look out at the valley. There was not even a pinprick of light to be seen. And when the first cock crowed she woke again, this time knowing that sleep was out of the question. She got up, dressed and slipped out.

The valley was quiet and even more peaceful than usual at this time of morning. It had a completely unspoiled feeling about it: she felt that no one had ever trodden it and never would. A light mist hovered over the fields, shrouding the trees, a mist that would lift in a very short time to let the heat come blazing through.

She passed the farm, saw that the shutters were opened in the downstairs rooms and knew her grandparents would be stirring. Her grandfather always got up at cock-crow. She went by and took the turning that led up the hill past the sunflower house. Their shutters were securely fastened; they must be sleeping still. She lingered for a while outside their gate gazing at the sunflowers and the house that they had loved over so many years. Their house: it had been. And now it was Christian's. She found that she did not mind that, and wished that Christian and his father would not sell. How nice it would be if they were to come back summer after summer and they could all meet again!

She went on up the hill to the church and took the back road, descending into the valley again by the other road, the one they had walked when they went on their picnic the other day. As she emerged from it she met Aunt Nicole.

They exclaimed at one another for being up so early. Simultaneously, they said that they had been unable to sleep.

"Walk a little way with me, Claudine."

They walked slowly, saying nothing at all to begin with, but enjoying the smells of the morning. The birds were in full throttle, singing from the highest trees. Aunt Nicole sighed, but it was a sigh of happiness.

"Claudine, I've a secret to tell you. Can you keep a secret?"

Claudine hesitated. Secrets were something that were beginning to weigh heavily. But she knew that this was one she could not refuse to accept. She nodded, knowing already what it was that her aunt would tell her.

"You know the professor – the German professor? Otto? Yes, I believe you do. You knew he was in the churchyard that day, didn't you? You know his son Christian." Aunt Nicole paused.

"We've become friendly with Christian. We like him very much."

"I hope I shall too. You see, Claudine – Otto and I are

going to be married."

"That's marvellous!" And it was, thought Claudine. How could it not be with Aunt Nicole smiling and happy, and Christian's father, who must be lonely in many ways, able at last to have the woman that he wanted? There was grandfather of course, but he had to be put out of mind at the moment. She hugged and kissed her aunt.

"We're telling no one else at present, Claudine, except for your mother and father. But I can't tell my father." Her eyes sobered. "You know the story? Well then, you will understand."

"But what can you do? You can't keep it from him for ever."

No, they could not, but they had decided that they would go away and be married in Heidelberg, and then, when, or if, it ever seemed suitable, they would let him know. They had decided that it would be best for Otto to leave in a day or so, she would stay for another week and then depart also.

"But that's dreadful," cried Claudine. "Christian will go away and you too! We've been looking forward to having you for a whole month."

"I know, dear, and I'm sorry. But there is nothing else we can do."

Claudine apologised, she should never have brought that up. She felt ashamed to be thinking of herself instead of them. It was their happiness that was important. Wasn't it why they had brought the two of them together? Why they had brought them together? She was not sure.

"I shall tell your mother this evening. And I think that Christian's father is telling him today."

Around mid-morning Aunt Nicole drove off in her car. The children went to the river and soon afterwards Christian appeared.

"Has your father gone out in his car?" asked Sophie.

He had, said Christian. Had he told Christian something special that morning? asked Claudine.

Christian grinned. "We will be related. I am pleased about that."

"We shall be kind of cousins, won't we?" said Sophie. "You will come to visit us in Edinburgh and we will come to visit you in Heidelberg."

That would be nice, thought Claudine, it would help make up for what was going to happen this summer. They had several weeks left and there would be no Christian and no Aunt Nicole. They had got used to the idea of meeting Christian every day: it would be odd without him. Empty. One more day, and then he and his father would be gone. His father still intended to sell the house; he had said that it would not be possible for them to come here, not with Nicole's father living at the farm below. Christian said too that his father had no grudge against their grandfather, none at all. As far as he was concerned, the past was dead and buried. But he did not expect the old man to accept him as a son-in-law now.

So there would only be one more day to spend together. One more day this year, but there would be many other days in other years, said Christian. To Claudine it was little consolation: she was too impatient to wait for other years.

"See you tomorrow!" they promised, when they parted at the end of the afternoon.

Claudine went off for a long walk alone further up the valley. She did not want company. Paul went to do the job that he had begun the day before, to finish repairing a fence. He liked doing this job, making the boundaries tight and secure so that the beasts would not stray. Sophie was left with nothing to do.

She ran into the farmhouse to get a drink. Both grandparents were sitting on the verandah having a cool drink themselves. *Grand-père* was a little tired, *Grand'mère* explained; he had decided to have a little rest before milking.

"And what have you been doing today, child?" asked *Grand'mère*.

"Playing with Christian," said Sophie, then stopped appalled, remembering that she was not supposed to pronounce his name either here or at home. It had slipped out so easily; they were used

103

to Christian now as part of the company.

"Christian? Who is that?" *Grand-père* sat up straight. "Is it the German boy?"

Sophie stuttered. She was bad at lying, unless well prepared in advance, and knew that she could not make a good job of it. Numbly, she admitted that it was. "But we weren't doing any harm, honest we weren't, *Grand-père*. And Christian is very nice. Not nasty at all."

Had they been in his house again? demanded her grandfather. Yes, she said, bleakly. And had they talked with his father? Only a little, faltered Sophie. And did the professor know that their Aunt Nicole was back staying here? Sophie nodded.

"*Mon Dieu!*"

"I am sure Nicole has not seen him though, Jean-Paul," said *Grand'mère*. "She has been away every day visiting friends. She has been very little in the valley. There has been no opportunity for her to see him."

Grand-père was staring at Sophie, searching her face, wanting to know the truth. Had Aunt Nicole met the professor? Well, had she? He demanded an answer. His voice thundered at her.

"I don't know," she faltered again, wishing she could run and hide in the damson wood. She would need to hide somewhere, after this. *Everyone* would be furious.

"You don't know!" roared her grandfather. "You do know! I can see it in your face."

His wife entreated him to be calm, not to get excited. He did not listen, he would not take his eyes from Sophie. She must tell him everything there was to be known. *Everything*.

Haltingly, she began. She could not do anything else, as she explained afterwards; it was like giving evidence under torture.

And so their grandfather discovered that his daughter was proposing to marry the German for whom he had gone to prison twenty-one years before.

11

Grand-père Goes to the Sunflower House

SOPHIE SAT HUDDLED in the hedge, petrified by what she had done. She didn't dare go up the hill and tell Claudine. She had seen her sister in the distance going up ahead of her. From where she sat she could see the farmhouse. The verandah was now empty.

The hedge was scratchy, it itched her arms and legs and caught at her hair. She watched a large insect crawling close to her sandalled foot. She thought that she would have to spend the night there, she would never be able to face them.

And then she lifted her head. *Grand-père* had come out on to the verandah wearing his blue cotton jacket. Then *Grand'mère* appeared, and she was talking to him. She was waving her hands about a lot for her. Normally they were at peace in her lap, or sometimes resting on her hips.

Grand-père was coming down the two steps from the verandah now on to the path below. He hastened towards the gate without glancing round, even though his wife was calling to him. Sophie could hear her calling. "Jean-Paul," she cried. "Jean-Paul, come back!" He did not even look back. "I am coming too then," she said.

At that he turned. "Do *not* come!" he thundered. Then he went through the gateway and out into the road.

Sophie knew at once where he would be heading. She listened

to the sound of his feet on the road gradually dying away. Then she could no longer hear them. And she could no longer see him: he was hidden by the hedges and the trees, and she guessed that he must have turned off to the right to go up the hill towards the sunflower house.

Grand'mère, her head bowed, went back into the house, and the ribboned curtain moved gently to and fro.

Sophie crawled out of her hiding-place and shot up the drive at full speed, scuffing her toes but not even feeling the pain. Claudine was lying on the terrace reading a book.

"Claudine," Sophie gasped. "Something terrible has happened. Come quickly!"

Claudine blinked, shading her eyes from the sun with her hand.

Sophie looked round cautiously but there was no sign of their parents. "It's to do with *Grand-père*. And the professor." That brought Claudine bolt upright. What did Sophie mean? Explain at once! Sophie, squatting close to her sister, did so. Claudine gazed at her, aghast.

"You stupid little –" She stopped. It was too serious to say any more. Something would have to be done.

They went first to search out Paul. They found him in the field next to the farmhouse.

"We will be too late," said Paul quietly, when he heard the news. "*Grand-père* is bound to be there by now."

There was always the chance, said Claudine, that Christian's father might not be at home. Perhaps he had not yet returned from his day's outing with Aunt Nicole. But Paul said that he had seen the little red Volkswagen passing half an hour before. And even as he spoke they saw a small green car coming along the road towards the farm.

They set off to the sunflower house. They waved to Aunt Nicole who waved back gaily, not knowing what was in store for her. At the turning off they met Christian. His face was grey, his eyes had a dazed, frightened look in them.

"You must fetch a doctor," he said, his voice breaking.

"A doctor!" shrieked Sophie. "Has *Grand-père* shot your father again?"

"Hush, Sophie." Paul put a hand on Christian's shoulder to stop him trembling. "What happened, Christian?"

Christian took a deep breath and swallowed deeply. He told them that their grandfather had arrived at the house; he had been very angry and begun to shout straight away. He had spoken very fast, and in French, and Christian had only been able to understand a few phrases here and there. But the gist of the matter was that the old man had been berating the professor for returning to disturb his valley, his family and his daughter. Had he not caused enough trouble in the past? Christian's father had said that he had come back to sell the house, that was all, and he had happened to meet Nicole.

At that, Claudine's gloom thickened and guilt swamped her.

"My father was calm," said Christian. "He did not shout back or try to make arguments."

"I can believe that," said Paul. "And I can believe too that *Grand-père* would shout and fume."

"What then?" asked Claudine.

"And then –" Christian gazed at them, full of misery. "And then your grandfather just collapsed. Like that. Like a pack of cards going down."

Claudine began to run up the hill towards the house; Paul went back down to the farm to tell his grandmother and telephone for the doctor. Sophie did not know what to do, which direction to go in; she fancied neither. She stayed with Christian, sliding her hand up into his. They stood in the road half-way between the two houses.

When Claudine arrived at the sunflower house, she found her grandfather lying on the floor, with Christian's father bathing his head.

"Paul has gone to phone for the doctor."

The professor nodded. They crouched beside her grandfather, saying nothing, watching the old man's face. He was alive, thank goodness! Claudine watched his chest moving gently up and down. But his face looked ghastly, a sort of bluish-purple under the brown skin.

Her grandmother arrived next, with Paul, Aunt Nicole and Christian. Aunt Nicole gave the professor a quick glance before turning to her father. Sophie had been sent to fetch their mother and father. *Grand'mère* went down at once on her knees and put her hands round her husband's face. She said nothing.

Almost immediately came their mother and father. The room was full of people. The professor rose, motioning to Christian to leave with him, and the other three children went also. They gathered in the garden where they sat in a row on the wooden bench in front of the sunflowers.

Shortly they heard a car in the road: the doctor was arriving. Bustling, carrying his squat black bag, he went past them with a quick "*Bonjour*" and into the house. Their father and Aunt Nicole came out. The latter went to the gate where she stood leaning on the top spar, with her back to the garden. The professor got up, eyed her in a helpless sort of way but did not go to her.

The doctor had ordered an ambulance before he came, so their grandfather was soon on his way to hospital at Villeneuve. He had had a heart attack, a serious one, and would need to be taken into the intensive care unit. It would be touch-and-go, was the doctor's opinion, but he was not a heart expert; it would be for the specialist to say.

The specialist said likewise.

Aunt Nicole and their mother spent the night at the farmhouse with their grandmother. The children spent the night with their father, and Christian with his father in their house. Sophie cowered in a corner of the sitting room crying off and on, although her father told her that it was not her fault that their grandfather had had a heart attack.

"Perhaps you didn't help any. But you mustn't blame yourself for it."

"It was all my fault," burst out Claudine. "I began it all. I was nosey, I had to push and pry until I uncovered everything."

But her father said that that was not true either, that it had all started a long long time ago. It had started even before twenty-one years ago when their Aunt Nicole had met the professor. It had started from the moment that Germany had invaded France, as far as their grandfather was concerned. Their father saw it all of a piece, whereas they could only see their little corner of it.

In the morning the news was a little more encouraging: *Grand-père* was holding his own. It did not sound too promising to Paul who had been praying for a miracle.

Aunt Nicole came to seek out Claudine. She looked pale, with mauve rings beneath her eyes, and she was no longer gay.

They walked in the damson wood. Claudine waited with apprehension for her aunt to speak. For a while she did not but walked, head bent, eyes cast down on the tangled undergrowth, and then she said, with a long sigh, "Oh, why can things never be simple?" It was not a question that required an answer. "I'm afraid that Otto and I shall have to part, Claudine. Again."

"No!"

"It looks as if we must. If Father dies and we marry now then we shall have that cloud over us. It would be a bad way to start a marriage."

"You would –" Claudine stopped. You would forget in time, she had wanted to say but could not for it would have sounded heartless and she did not feel heartless about her grandfather. More than anything else she felt confusion. "He may live," she said.

"And then if we went ahead we might kill him. I caused enough trouble twenty-one years ago. I was young and wilful –"

"But perhaps you were right," cried Claudine.

"Too much trouble came of it for me to have been right. I should have listened to my father then."

"I don't see that. What he wanted of you was wrong."

"In your eyes, Claudine, not his. And you see, every decision we take affects others, sends out ripples to touch them. If I married Otto it would affect many people. I must give him up, and this time for good. I don't want to –" And then she concluded with an effort, "but I think I have to."

"But it's terrible! You love him and he loves you."

"But could we be happy together if my father died? Could we? Do you think it would be possible, Claudine?"

Claudine looked into her aunt's amber-coloured eyes which normally were so full of amusement and pleasure and now ached with pain. She had to turn away.

"Forgive me, I shouldn't ask you such terrible questions."

Aunt Nicole touched her lightly on the shoulder and then was gone, running and stumbling through the wood.

It rained that day, fortunately: the sun would have been too much. The rain was more in keeping with their mood. They walked, regardless of it, across their grandfather's fields and picked their way through dripping wet woods. The moist green world was bearable. The house was impossible. Their mother's eyes were full of gentle reproach, all the worse because it was gentle. They would have preferred one of her torrents and to be told that they were the most selfish and thoughtless children any woman had the misfortune to bear. No one was blaming them outright for anything, except themselves.

They gravitated towards their stretch of river, found Christian there sitting on a fallen tree watching the rain dance on the water. He had heard of Aunt Nicole's decision.

They sat in a row on the trunk, and overhead rain pattered on the branches of the trees, sending down drops every now and then to plop on their heads. It was soft, quiet rain, slightly hypnotic, quite different from the downpours that had followed the storms. It was good fishing weather, thought Paul, wishing that his biggest worry that day might be whether he would catch anything or not.

"Do you think they're doing the right thing, Christian?" asked Claudine. "Parting? Paul does. But then he's all for the quiet life."

"That's not fair," Paul retorted angrily. "I'm thinking of *Grand-père*. I want him to have a life, whether it is quiet or not."

"But Aunt Nicole and Christian's father deserve a life too. And together, if that's what they want."

"I think Claudine is right," said Christian.

He is not your grandfather, thought Paul, but did not say so.

"I do too," said Sophie, pulling her anorak hood further over her face. "I want them to get married."

"Aunt Nicole is still quite young," said Claudine. "She has a long time yet but *Grand-père* might —"

"Die," finished Paul.

They listened again to the hiss of the rain and stared at the pearls of water trembling on the edges of the leaves.

"It is for them to decide," said Christian.

"I suppose," said Claudine. "But — well, perhaps they need a gentle push."

"We're not going to do any more pushing," said Paul, alarmed. "We've done enough. Too much!"

Perhaps, thought Claudine, but she had a strange feeling that there was still some part for them to play, that she could not quite put into words. They *were* involved. And Aunt Nicole had talked of ripples touching people. Like them. The four of them. Claudine thought that Aunt Nicole had been appealing to her in the wood; she had seemed to feel that Claudine would understand. And she thought too that her aunt felt far from certain about her decision.

"Christian's father is lonely, isn't that right? And Aunt Nicole must be too sometimes in spite of her career. Why should they be kept apart by *Grand-père's* silliness. Yes, silliness!"

It was not silliness, Paul informed her curtly; they knew that their grandfather's feelings ran deep. All right, all right, she knew all that, they had heard it since they could crawl, and she, for one, was sick of it. Aunt Nicole was not proposing to marry his brother's murderer. She was very fond of her grandfather but that did not mean that she had to be fond of his likes or dislikes, did it?

Paul shrugged.

"I want them to marry," said Sophie again.

"And you, Christian?"

He nodded.

"Paul?"

Paul did not take his eyes off the river. It was running more fully today between the green banks, and he was wishing that he was downstream, alone. The river looked so free and unbothered. He felt that he would never be that way himself again.

"Paul?"

"Oh, no doubt you're all right. *Grand-père* is old and they are not. It doesn't seem right that they should have to make such a sacrifice. Yes, I admit it! Are you satisfied now, Claudine?"

She ignored his last sentence. She said, "Well, then, I think we should let them know how we feel. I think we should tell them that we have discussed it fully and come to the conclusion that they are entitled to go ahead and marry if they choose, in spite of everything."

In spite of what had happened, and might happen, to their grandfather.

The Snake Reappears

"I CANNOT KILL my father, Claudine."

"You don't know that it would kill him. He needn't know. You could go away."

Aunt Nicole was scanning the hillside with the church on top, which was blurred this morning by a steady drizzle of rain. It had rained all night. Her eyebrows were drawn close together. Her father's condition had taken a turn for the better and the doctor was more hopeful. He said that it was early days yet to predict but the old man was tough and he thought there was a fair chance he would make a recovery, given a bit of luck and peace and quiet. Above all, he must not be allowed to get excited. Above all, he must not be allowed to meet up with the German professor again.

"I sounded Mother and Father out and they said they'd like to see you happy too. They thought you deserved it."

"They did?" There was a hint of eagerness in that response, thought Claudine.

"Not that they would ever say so to you probably. They feel they shouldn't interfere."

"Whereas you —" Aunt Nicole even smiled a little.

"It's just that we feel strongly about it. Very. And you talked about ripples, Aunt Nicole. Well, they're touching us, Paul and Sophie and me, and Christian. It seems such a waste!"

She nodded, almost absent-mindedly.

"If I were you I would certainly do it."

She smiled with her eyes now. She said that she did not doubt that for one minute. But it was unlikely that Claudine's father would ever act in the same way as hers: he was of a different generation with different expectations as regards his children.

"And your father has very few prejudices, Claudine. Although we all have our own little bits and pieces. But don't forget that your father has never had the kind of experiences that mine had. And pray God he never will!"

"Even *Grand'mère* might not be against the professor, if she weren't afraid for *Grand-père*."

Aunt Nicole nodded. Years ago, at the time of her first meeting with Otto, her mother had said that she had nothing against their friendship, except her husband's objection. But that was enough for her.

Aunt Nicole was much calmer today; the desperation of yesterday was gone. Claudine supposed that she had got over the initial shock and was able to see things more in the round, to take a longer view perhaps?

She said that she was going to go for a long walk. She set off along the road that led further up the valley.

Claudine went up the hill towards the sunflower house. The shutters had been opened and flung back. She hovered around in the roadway where she could be seen and before long Christian came out munching a long piece of bread. He joined her and together they walked up to the church. They went into the churchyard and wandered amongst the graves and Claudine pointed out those of her ancestors. They stopped in front of her grandfather's brother's grave, the one who had been executed by the Germans.

'Hero of the Resistance . . .'

They read his epitaph and moved on.

Christian had spoken to his father about their conversation at the river. He had said that he would think again, he was still thinking, had never ceased to, but it was a very big decision to take when someone else's life was involved. Also, he thought that perhaps it had to be Nicole's decision more than his since it was her father who was involved. It was a big responsibility for her.

Claudine's throat felt suddenly dry.

"I said at least he should speak to her again, try to persuade her."

The rain had stopped, the sun was coming out to flood the valley and dry up the roads and fields. Birds were carolling in the yews high overhead as if celebrating the return of the sun.

From up here on the hill they could look down on Christian's house, see the roof and the trees around and the strip of roadway in front. They were watching carefully. After a little while they saw Christian's father come out of the gate and go down the hill.

"Do you think?" Claudine looked at Christian.

"Perhaps."

They left the churchyard and went down to the house. They sat on the bench in front of the sunflowers.

"Would you like a drink?" asked Christian. "Something to eat?"

She shook her head; she did not want anything but to sit here and wait. There was nothing more to do now but that.

They heard Sophie approaching, her high voice twittering, like the birds, as she chattered to Paul. They looked cautiously round the gate and, seeing Christian and Claudine, came into the garden. Sophie rushed forward excitedly.

"They've met one another. We saw them. They are walking together along the road."

"I had to drag her away. Otherwise she would have followed them. She will have to get a job in a detective agency when she grows up. She is a natural."

"I just like to know what's happening, that's all. Like Claudine." Sophie smiled, then squatted down on the ground in front of the flowers. Her head was circled with yellow.

Tomorrow, thought Paul, I will go and work for the whole day in the fields from early morning till late at night, so that I will come home exhausted. It was a good feeling, to come home dead tired after a full day's work in the open air. Your mind then didn't think about anything, didn't keep picking over worries. He needed such a day.

If Aunt Nicole does marry Christian's father, thought Claudine, then I won't be able to go to Paris and stay with her any more. It would be disappointing not to be able to go and live on the Left Bank as she had planned and hoped: it would be the end of that particular dream. Unless she were to go alone. That would need rethinking.

If Aunt Nicole marries Christian's father, thought Sophie, perhaps I shall be a bridesmaid. She would like a yellow dress, the colour of the sunflowers, and a head-dress of small yellow sunflowers like the virgins at that temple had had. And she would carry a bunch of white roses.

If my father marries their aunt, thought Christian, then they will come to visit us in Heidelberg and he would go back to visit them in Edinburgh, at Festival time, when the city was alive and full of interesting things. Claudine had told him all about it. His life would change quite a lot if their Aunt Nicole was to become his stepmother. Some of the changes he might like, and others he might not. He could not quite imagine what it would be like.

The church bell began to toll above them and the air seemed to vibrate. They cocked their heads to listen, and soundlessly, counted the strokes.

"Twelve," said Claudine with satisfaction, as the last stroke died away.

The valley was quiet again.

"They're taking a long time," said Sophie, scratching the bites on her legs with both hands.

Naturally, said Claudine, they were taking a decision that would affect the rest of their lives. Who would not take a long time?

"I expect when you decide to get married you'll do it in a flash," said Paul.

Claudine blushed and glared at her brother. She informed him that she had no intentions of getting married, she intended to lead her own life. He muttered that he did not know then why she was so anxious then to push other people into it.

Sophie got up and went to the gate. She hung over it, watching the road up from the valley. The morning seemed one of the longest that she could ever remember. The minutes dragged by, hot and slow, and she almost felt that she could see them move. If she said so to Claudine she would laugh at her. Claudine would say that it was not possible to see minutes passing, but Sophie felt that she could.

"You'll fall over the top of the gate if you're not careful," said Paul.

She was leaning further and further over, watching the ground, and every now and then she saw a little furry caterpillar crawl by. And then came a column of ants marching in a thick column as if they were going to war. Sophie liked watching ants from a distance, hated them when they were crawling all over their draining board. They waged a continuous battle to keep the ants at bay in the house.

Suddenly, she caught a movement out of the corner of her eye, and almost fell right over the gate on to her head. Squawking loudly, she recovered balance and landed back in the garden.

"They're coming!"

"Don't shout," said Claudine. "What a racket you make, Sophie! And come and sit down. We must look as if we're simply sitting here concerned with our own affairs. We mustn't look as if we've been waiting for them."

Paul snorted. "They're not daft, you know."

Aunt Nicole and the professor arrived at the gate. For a moment they looked startled when they saw the four children sitting in a line on the bench. And then Aunt Nicole laughed.

"I might have known," she said, coming down the steps into the garden. "I think you four have been hatching plots."

They did not answer, they were waiting to be told the news. For there was news to be told, that was obvious. The professor was smiling. He stood in the middle of the garden looking at them, and then he turned to Aunt Nicole.

"Shall we tell them, Nicole?"

"I think so." She too was smiling. "But it must be a real secret this time, you understand."

They nodded.

The professor went to Aunt Nicole and put an arm around her shoulders. "We have decided to get married after all."

Sophie jumped up and shrieked with delight. But Aunt Nicole said that although of course they were very happy about it, they were sad too. Understandably. Because of her father. She wished so much . . . She sighed. They had to be realistic, she said, and know what was possible. They would not be able to tell him and that was not a very happy situation – she disliked having to be deceitful – but it was the only thing to be done. The professor was going to leave the following day taking Christian with him, and in two weeks' time Aunt Nicole would follow to Heidelberg, where they would marry. They both felt they wanted to waste no more time; so much had been wasted already. It would be a quiet wedding, with only Christian and one or two close friends of the professor's present, and, they hoped, the children's mother. She would be able to give some excuse to go away for a few days, but their father would have to remain with them in the valley.

"Won't we be there then?" asked Sophie, filled with disappointment, the vision of herself in yellow carrying white flowers fading rapidly. "I want to see you married. I want to be a bridesmaid. I've never been a bridesmaid."

Aunt Nicole said gently that she would love to have them all there, nothing would please her more, but it would not be possible. It might arouse suspicion if they were all to depart, and someone had to stay to with their grandparents. Also, everything must be done to keep the news from their grandfather. Eventually they hoped it might be possible to break it to him, but he would have to be prepared first, very gradually, and they would have to be sure that his health would stand it. If not, they would not tell him; Aunt Nicole would come back to the valley alone from time to time, as she had always done.

"So Christian will not be able to come here?" said Claudine slowly.

"He will come some day," said the professor. "And now, I am going to open some wine. We will have a celebration."

He fetched two bottles of ice-cold sparkling rosé wine from the fridge. The first cork went up into the air like a rocket and landed in the middle of the sunflowers. Sophie ran to retrieve it, declaring that she would keep it for ever, as a souvenir. The wine, shimmering in the glasses, smelled sweet and fragrant. The two boys looked at one another. Someone should propose a toast and it should be one of them.

"To Aunt Nicole," said Paul, raising his glass.

"And my father," finished Christian.

They raised their glasses and drank.

"That's gorgeous," said Sophie. She had a kind of swooning feeling after the first sip.

Aunt Nicole and the professor now raised their glasses and drank to one another. Down in the valley, thought Claudine, their grandmother was sitting alone in the farmhouse, she who should have been here to drink her daughter's health but could not. And in the hospital, thought Paul, lay their grandfather still hovering on a fine line between life and death, as if on a tightrope, with no net to catch him if he fell. Paul could almost feel him on that rope. He gulped another mouthful of wine. Would *Grand-père* ever be properly well again, would he be able to look after the farm for another four years? It seemed to Paul that his own future was less certain now, for if his grandfather were to die or not be able to keep on the farm then who would look after it? This summer had been full of change, and usually the summers had been almost identical, one following the other like beads on a string. They had come back to find the same things and the same people in the same places and watch the fruit ripen and the corn grow yellow in the fields. There had never been a summer such as this before.

The wine is going to my head, thought Claudine, as she let the heavy, musky liquid trickle over her throat. To drink wine in the heat of the day with little food inside you was no doubt bad, but this was a funny mixed-up day and they were doing funny mixed-up things. They would be happy, Aunt Nicole and Christian's father; at least, she thought so. But what if *Grand-père* were to find out and die as a result? She put the thought out of her mind at once; it was a thought not to be tolerated. But even as she was banishing it she had a sudden flash of insight and knew that her aunt and Otto Brander had faced up to the fact that he might die; they were not pretending it could not happen.

Sophie drained her glass, tilting it upside down. She said that she loved wine, especially when it was fizzy and sparkled, and she wished she could drink it all day long. The professor, laughing, poured a little more into her glass.

So there was to be another secret, thought Claudine. Secrets were really only a matter of not being able to tell everyone everything all of the time. Complete truth was not possible, or desirable. She felt very solemn as she sat there thinking solemn thoughts.

"The snake!" whispered Sophie suddenly, pointing.

They turned, and saw, emerging from the sunflowers, a brown and yellow striped snake. It was moving slowly but steadily towards the house.

"Stay still," said the professor, "but get out of its way if you have to of course."

He went inside, to re-emerge with the broom. In front of the door he paused to see that the snake was still travelling towards the house, towards his feet on the doorstep. Sophie put both hands over her mouth. The others, transfixed like statues, held their breath, and watched the snake and the professor.

Closer, closer, it slithered, writhing slightly from side to side, and now it was only two feet from his bare, sandalled feet.

Swiftly, and without a blink of hesitation, he brought the end of the broom down right across the snake's back. There was a sickening smack, and both Sophie and Claudine turned away. When they looked back, they saw the professor carrying the broken snake over the broom handle towards the side of the garden. He threw it clean over the top of the hedge into the field. Claudine remembered from somewhere — was it *Huckleberry Finn*? — that when a snake died its mate came seeking its body.

"Sorry I had to do that," said the professor, as he came back and propped the broom against the wall. He grimaced. "I wouldn't have killed it if I hadn't had to. But we couldn't have had it inside the house."

"You were very brave," said Sophie, her eyes large.

He shook his head. "Not really. I had no choice."

Aunt Nicole, who had turned very pale whilst he was confronting the snake, went to him and slipped her hand into his. "We've something else to tell them, haven't we, Otto? About the house."

"Yes, indeed. We have decided to keep it."

"Hurrah!" shouted Sophie.

"We shall have to close it up again in the meantime of course. But one day . . . well, who knows?"

One day he and Aunt Nicole and Christian would be able to come back and spend a summer in it. Perhaps not for a long time. Perhaps not until their grandfather died. He did not say that but must have thought it, as they did.

"There is one thing," said Claudine.

"And what is that?"

"Do you think you could change the name? 'Mon Repos' is so awful." He murmured agreement. "Could you call it 'Les Tournesols'?"

He did not see why not. It would be much more suitable. Would everyone prefer that? There were choruses of assent.

"It is amazing how the sunflowers have survived all these years. I must admit I did not expect to see them."

"We've always been a bit surprised too," said Paul. "They must just keep seeding themselves."

Aunt Nicole gave a little laugh, slightly sheepish. "I have a confession to make."

"Indeed?" said the professor, mock-seriously.

'*I* have kept planting the sunflowers."

"You?" cried Sophie and Claudine together.

"Yes, I. Every spring, when I came to visit my parents. It was easy to work away in here unnoticed — it is so well screened from the road. I couldn't bear to think of the garden without sunflowers. You always said they had made you fall in love with the house, Otto."

He took her hand. He said, with a smile, "I call that an act of faith."

The look between them was so intensely private that the children had to turn away. They stood gazing at the house, its honey-coloured stone burnished by the late-afternoon sun. It would have to be shut up again, that they accepted, but they would be able to come back, summer after summer, and sit amongst the sunflowers, as they had always done. And one day Christian would join them. But above all, it was an immense relief to know that the house was not going to pass into the hands of strangers, that it would remain within the circle of the family.